"Nick, I have a confession."

Grace decided that since this was a game of Truth or Dare she'd just tell him the truth. "Do you see those women over there?" She pointed to her friends. They all stared back as if they were watching a bad reality-TV show. "They dared me to come over here and give you something."

Nick grinned. "Like what?"

"Like my underwear."

He didn't look the slightest bit surprised. She guessed women offered him their underwear on a pretty regular basis. She sidled closer, dangling her panties in front of him so the girls could see.

Nick gave her panties an appraising look. Then he grabbed her around the waist and pulled her close. "Wanna give your friends something better to watch?"

Oh, my.

The DJ was playing The Cure's "Just Like Heaven," and the beat reverberated through the bar beneath her elbow. Nick's lips were mere inches away.

What was it the Romans used to say?

Oh, yeah. Carpe diem.

Donna Birdsell

Donna Birdsell lives near Philadelphia, where she absolutely doesn't get any of her ideas from her perfectly normal family, friends and neighbors.

She's addicted to reality television and chocolate, loves a good snowstorm and cooks to relax.

She spent many years writing press releases, newsletters and marketing brochures until a pregnancy complication kept her home from the office. She needed something to keep her busy, so she started her very first novel.

Five years later her dream of becoming a published fiction author came true when *The Painted Rose*, her first historical romance, was released.

She is excited about this, her first book for Harlequin NEXT.

You can reach Donna through her Web site at www.DonnaBirdsell.com.

Donna Birdsell

Suburban Secrets

SUBURBAN SECRETS

Copyright © 2006 by Donna Birdsell

isbn-13:978-0-373-88110-9

isbn-10:   0-373-88110-X

TheNextNovel.com

PRINTED IN U.S.A.

To all the girls who kept my secrets.
We sure had some good times, didn't we?

CHAPTER 1

Friday, 7:17 a.m.
Weird Eggs

"Kevin, let's move! It's 7:17."

From the bottom of the stairs, Grace Becker heard the telltale thump of a body rolling out of bed. *Jesus.* They had thirteen minutes. She'd better find something he could eat on the way to school.

Megan and Callie were already in the kitchen, poking the food around on their plates.

"Finish your eggs," Grace said.

Callie stuck out her tongue. "What's *in* them?"

"Camembert and shallots," said Grace. "Why? Don't you like it?"

"What's wrong?" said Megan.

"What do you mean, what's wrong?" Grace grabbed a Pop-Tart from the pantry and stuck it in the toaster.

"You always cook weird stuff when you're upset," Megan said. "So, what's wrong?"

Grace bit the inside of her cheek. What was she supposed to say?

Well, girls, I'm upset because your father left me for his older, less attractive assistant; he's been a complete dirtbag about the divorce; we're probably going to lose our house; and the closest thing Mommy's had to a date in the last ten months was drinking a Dixie cup of warm Gatorade with your field hockey coach, Ludmilla?

She sighed. "Nothing's wrong. Eat your breakfast."

"Mom, nobody eats breakfast. And I mean *nobody*." Megan, at twelve, had some sort of detailed list in her head about what everyone did or did not do, which she checked with agonizing frequency.

"They especially don't eat *eggs* for breakfast," Callie added.

"Yeah?" said Grace. "When I was your age, I would have killed to have eggs for breakfast. But it was cold cereal and a vitamin pill everyday for me. Grandma actually had a job."

"*You* could get a job," Callie suggested.

"Be careful what you wish for." Grace tried to draw a deep breath, but it got stuck halfway down.

She *was* going to have to get a job. But where? She hadn't held a position outside her yoga class in thirteen years.

8

Everything in her life had revolved around Tom, his career and their kids. His bosses had loved her, his coworkers' wives had envied her, and his clients had jockeyed for invitations to Becker parties. She'd been the events coordinator, secretary, moral support beam, taxi service and butt kisser extraordinaire, all without ever drawing a paycheck.

But it was time to face facts. Tom was gone. He was making a new life, with a new woman who would be all those things.

So who would *she* be now?

She forced a smile. "If I get a job, who'll take care of you guys?"

Megan rolled her eyes. "Please, Mom. I'm almost thirteen. I think I can get my own breakfast."

"What? A handful of grapes and a Diet Coke? I don't think so. You're going to have a decent breakfast if I have to give it to you through an IV. You're not going to end up looking like Lara Flynn Boyle."

"Who?" said Callie.

"The walking corpse on *Twin Peaks*."

"Twin *what*?"

"Never mind. Eat your eggs."

"I'm with Callie. I think you should get a job," said Megan. "You need a change. Don't you want some excitement?"

"There's plenty of excitement around here," Grace said. "Just yesterday while I was folding towels in the laundry room, I saw Mrs. Pollack's dog bite the mailman in the crotch."

"Mother!" Megan jerked her head in Callie's direction. "Was that really an appropriate thing to say in front of the child?"

"Who are you calling a child?" Callie shouted. "I'm almost nine!"

The Pop-Tart started smoking in the toaster just as Kevin flew into the kitchen and slid across the floor in his socks. "Four minutes!" he said, breathlessly.

"Wow, you can hardly tell," Megan said.

Grace examined her son. His hair stuck out from his head like he'd spent the night in electroshock therapy. His shirt was wrinkled, and she was pretty sure he'd taken the jeans he was wearing out of the hamper.

"No way. Get up there and do it right," she said. "Meet us at the car in—" she checked her watch "—three minutes. I'll have your breakfast with me."

"Why can't I have a Pop-Tart, too?" Callie whined. "You only get something good around here if you're late."

"Is Dad coming to my game this afternoon?" Megan asked.

"I'm sure he is, but I'll ask him when I see him."

She'd be seeing him this morning. Damned Tom and

his damned lawyer. Big Prick and Bigger Prick, as she liked to think of them.

They'd scheduled the fifth meeting in two weeks to discuss the settlement. This divorce was such a joke, all they needed to get it onto network TV was a laugh track.

Grace plucked the molten hot Pop-Tart from the toaster and wrapped it in a paper towel. "Okay, let's roll. We have seven minutes to get you to school."

The girls happily dumped the rest of their eggs down the garbage disposal and grabbed their backpacks from the hooks by the door.

Friday, 8:25 a.m.
Foot Powder and the Mouth

The Grocery King piped a Muzak version of U2's "Sunday Bloody Sunday" into the aisles. Grace was just the age to find this both entertaining and disturbing.

She checked her list.

Salmon. Fresh dill. New potatoes. She was going to make herself something special tomorrow night to celebrate her freedom. Her parents were taking the kids for the Columbus Day long weekend and solemnly swore to get them to all extracurricular activities on time and dressed in the correct uniforms.

Maybe it would be good to have a relaxing weekend

alone. Completely alone. She could think about what she was going to do with her life when she was the ex–Mrs. Thomas Becker.

The thought made her break into hives.

She hung a left into the pharmacy aisle and threw things into her cart.

She stopped in front of the Dr. Scholl's display. A lump crept up her throat, and before she could stop them, the tears came. She couldn't believe she hadn't had to buy foot powder in ten months.

Tom had notoriously damp feet. And it wasn't as though she missed his feet—they really were gross—but she'd loved him so much, she'd been able to overlook the grossness. Would she ever feel that way about someone's feet again?

As she fished through her purse for a tissue, she felt a hand on her shoulder. It was Lorraine Dobbs, otherwise known as the Mouth of South Whitpain.

"Grace? Are you alright?"

Grace nodded. Her blouse, now soaked with tears, stuck to her chest. "I think I'm allergic to foot powder."

Lorraine gave her a funny look. "O-*kay*, then. Are you going to Misty's later?"

Grace nodded again.

"Alrighty. See you there." Lorraine hurried off, one of the wheels on her cart shuddering in time with the Muzak version of "Rock the Casbah."

Grace checked her watch. Already nine minutes over her scheduled grocery shopping time.

Friday, 9:33 a.m.
Poster Girl

"We were about to send out the National Guard," said Tammy Lynn. "You're three minutes late."

"I know. I'm *so* sorry." Grace threw her coat and purse on a hook in the closet and rushed over to the chair at Tammy Lynn's station at Beautific, the salon where Grace had been getting her hair done for the past ten years.

"Grace, I'm only kidding," Tammy Lynn said, laughing, as she fastened the black polyester cape around Grace's neck.

"Right." Grace laughed with her.

But the thing was, she didn't *really* think it was funny. Punctuality was important. A minute here, two minutes there. They all added up. When you had three kids you learned how to manage your time, or else dinner was chronically late, homework time was chronically late, and you ended up cleaning the bathroom at ten-thirty at night instead of watching the rerun of *Murphy Brown* on Lifetime you'd been looking forward to all day.

Her shoulder muscles bunched painfully. She had to

relax. Maybe she could squeeze a few minutes of meditation in before lunch.

"Cover the gray and trim the ends?" Tammy Lynn asked, plucking the barrette from Grace's shoulder-length, brown hair.

"Mmm-hmm."

Tammy Lynn spun the chair around to face a poster of a slender, sophisticated woman with a soft, blond, bouncy cut that looked like at least twenty minutes worth of work every morning.

"Wait," Grace said. "I want that."

Tammy Lynn stopped the color bottle in midair. "What? The do on the poster?"

Grace nodded.

"Really? You sure? You gotta blow it out with a brush and curl it. You can't just put it back in a barrette."

Grace studied the poster again.

It wouldn't be a completely off-the-wall thing to do. She'd been blond once, a long, long time ago. Before Tom had hinted it wasn't quite sophisticated. Not quite who he thought she should be.

Maybe Megan was right. Maybe she needed to shake up her life a little. Hell, she could get up a few minutes earlier.

"Do it," she said.

Friday, 10:58 a.m.
Big and Bigger

As Grace waited for the elevator in the four-story, brick-and-tinted-window building that served as sub-urban Philadelphia's answer to the high-rise, she raked the wispy hairs at her neck with her fingernails.

What had she been thinking? She felt naked without her ponytail. And the last thing she wanted to feel around the man who was almost her ex-husband was naked.

She hadn't actually wanted to *be* naked around him, either, for a long time.

She supposed she had a sixth sense that he'd been cheating on her, which was probably why she'd skipped the meeting with the decorator that day and gone straight home, only to find Tom stretched out on their bed, covered with peanut butter. His assistant, Marlene, was on top of him, wearing nothing but a Smucker's negligee. A nauseating sight, considering that on her best day, wearing her best Donna Karan power suit, Marlene looked a lot like a broomstick in a red wig.

Grace had been angry as hell. In retrospect, she realized it was mostly because they'd ruined a pair of really good sheets, but also a little bit because she'd been married to Tom for thirteen years and they'd never made a PB&J sandwich together. The most creative thing they'd ever done in bed was fill out their taxes.

She supposed part of it was her own fault. Tom knew she lived and died by her Day-Timer, and if the Day-Timer said she'd be at the decorator's at two o'clock, then that's where she'd be.

If she'd been a tad more unpredictable, maybe they'd have had "lunch" at Marlene's place instead, and ruined *her* good sheets.

Grace stepped out of the elevator on the fourth floor at Kemper Ivy Kemper, where Tom's lawyer, aka Bigger Prick, practiced. The receptionist directed her to the conference room, where Big Prick, Bigger Prick and Grace's own lawyer, Debra Coyle, waited.

Tom raked his long fingers through salt-and-pepper hair. She could see the tension in his squared jaw. His bone structure was impeccable, really. He would undoubtedly age like Sean Connery, remaining breathtakingly handsome well into his retirement days.

She took a deep breath and pushed the door open.

Big Prick's eyes bugged. "You cut your hair. And it's *blond*."

Bigger Prick flashed his client a look.

Grace felt a moment of grateful relief before she considered where the compliment had come from. She gave

Tom a bitchy look. "I'm getting the kids' hair cut, too. I figure we'll save money on shampoo."

"Oh for God's sake, Grace. You know the children will be well taken care of, and—"

"Just hold on, Tom," his lawyer interrupted. "Debra, will you keep your client quiet for a few minutes?"

"I think she has every right to be pissed, David. Don't you?" Debra motioned to the chair next to hers, and Grace took a seat. "How many times are we going to rehash this pathetic settlement?"

"She signed a prenup, Debra."

"Then what are we doing here?"

"My client just wants to be fair. He wants to do what's right."

Grace snorted. "He should have thought of that before he decided to audition for the role of mascot for Skippy's porn division."

Tom pushed away from the table and stormed out the door.

Grace rubbed her temples. "Can we just get this over with?"

Bigger Prick slid the latest draft of the divorce settlement across the wide conference room table.

"Will you leave us alone for a few minutes?" Debra asked Bigger.

The other lawyer nodded and followed Tom from the

room. Grace could see them through the floor-to-ceiling windows, waiting just outside the door.

Upon closer inspection, Tom didn't look well. The bags under his eyes matched the gray suit he was wearing. Maybe the strain of the divorce was catching up to him, too.

Yeah, right. More likely he and Marlene had been dressing up in condiments all night.

A vision of Marlene's bony ass, covered in ketchup, flashed in Grace's mind. *Blech.*

"Grace, I don't think we're going to do much better than this," Debra said. "The terms are shitty, but you did sign a prenup. He gets all property and monies generated by his inheritance, including the house. You get half of what you've both made since you got married."

"You mean half of what *he's* made. He wouldn't let me work, Debra. God, I was so stupid."

Debra reached out and squeezed Grace's hand. "The child support is good. Some would argue that he's being generous."

"Generous? Listen, I don't give a crap about the money. Well, okay, maybe a small crap. But I'm going to lose the *house.* My *kids* are going to lose their house."

"Maybe you could offer to buy him out."

"How? The house is worth three-quarters of a million dollars."

Debra thought for a minute. "Can you borrow it from your parents?"

Grace shook her head. "They don't have that kind of money."

"Do you have anything you can sell? What about stocks? Jewelry?"

She shook her head. "It wouldn't be enough to buy him out." For the second time that day, tears threatened.

She'd worked so hard to make that house a home for Tom and the kids. It was a gorgeous, historic colonial manor house, once owned by William Penn's sous-chef or something. When they'd moved in, it was hardly more than an old pile of bricks. She'd restored it, room by room, over the years, finding authentic fixtures at flea markets and on the Internet. She loved that house, and now she'd never even be able to afford the taxes. But there were more important things than houses.

At least she'd won custody of the kids. Probably because—unlike the house—Marlene didn't want them.

"Screw it," she said. "Give me the papers."

"Are you sure?"

"I'm sure." She signed the papers, and Debra waved Tom and his lawyer back into the room.

"You did the right thing, Grace," Bigger Prick said. "The sooner we end this hostility, the sooner you and Tom can get on with your lives."

Right. Only now, hers would be almost unrecognizable.

Grace rose. "Good luck with Marlene."

Bigger Prick stuck out his hand. Grace ignored it.

She made it to the door before Tom said, "Wait, Grace. I want to talk to you. Alone."

Both lawyers looked stricken. But Grace nodded, and Tom held the door open for her as they left.

"What?" she said. "You want to thank me for signing that piece of shit agreement?"

He came closer. "No. I want to ask a favor of you."

"A *favor*?" She laughed. "You haven't changed a bit, have you?"

Tom closed the distance between them and guided her to an alcove in the lobby. "I need you to do something for me. In return, maybe we could work something out with the house."

She looked into his eyes. "You're serious?"

"Yes." He lowered his voice. "I need you to sign some papers."

"What kind of papers?"

"Work-related stuff."

She narrowed her eyes. "Why would you want *me* to sign work-related papers?"

He reached out, almost touching her hand before pulling back. He whispered, "Not *your* name."

Her insides went liquid. "No-oh. No way. Forget it."

Now he grabbed her hand. His voice was low and quick. Persuasive. His sales voice. "Come on, Gracie. You're the only one I know who can do this for me. You're the best."

"Are you crazy?" Her voice rose, and she made a concerted effort to quiet herself. "Are you nuts? Do you want to send me back to jail?"

"You won't get caught. I promise. It's a one-time deal."

She pulled her hand from his.

"Think about it, Gracie. Five minutes of your time and the house is yours."

"What about Marlene? I thought she wanted the house."

"Yeah, well. She'll just have to live without it."

He must have known how tempting this all would sound to her. He'd always been a great salesman, finding just the right carrot for the mules.

He'd found hers, alright. But it wasn't a big enough carrot.

"I'd want the 'Vette, too," she said. Tom's white 1976 Corvette was basically a fifteen-foot extension of his penis.

He frowned. "Grace—"

"Okay, then." She started walking toward the elevator, and he grabbed her arm.

"Wait. Alright. The 'Vette, too."

She realized then that he was really, truly desperate.

21

She chewed the inside of her cheek. "I'll think about it."

"Think fast, okay? I need this done quickly."

She nodded.

Before she could figure out what his intentions were, he leaned in and kissed her. "I'll call you."

She got almost to the elevator before she remembered to ask him about Megan's field hockey game.

"Hey," she shouted over her shoulder. "You know Megan has a game today?"

"Of course. I'll be there," he said. "I wouldn't miss it."

Grace walked out of the building and into the sunshine. She'd made a decision.

She didn't need meditation. She needed a margarita.

CHAPTER 1.5

Friday, 11:45 a.m.
Wild Card

Pete Slade popped another Tums and stared out the window of the Melrose Diner in South Philly. He had a bad feeling.

Hell, he'd had a bad feeling since this whole mess began. And the fact that he now had to rely on a sharp-looking kid with a hundred-dollar haircut and a different girl for every night of the week didn't help matters.

Nick Balboa wasn't what you'd call reliable. Not even a little bit. He was a low-level thug with big plans.

A wild card.

And he was gonna screw everything up.

Pete chugged his coffee and threw a couple bucks down on the table for the waitress.

Out on the street, he flipped open his cell phone and called Lou.

"Hey. I got a funny feeling."

"Yeah?" said Lou.

"Yeah. I'm gonna swing by the airport, maybe watch Balboa's car."

He imagined Lou rolling his eyes. But Pete had been doing this long enough to know when to follow his gut. Even when it was rebelling against him.

"Anything you want me to do?" Lou asked.

"Just sit tight. I'll call you if I need you."

Pete disconnected the call and popped another Tums. Jesus, he couldn't wait for this to be over.

CHAPTER 2

Friday, 11:56 a.m.
Grazing

Beruglia's was packed, as usual. Businessmen in athletic-cut suits lined the bar, hunched over low-carb beers and plates of South Beach–acceptable protein. Groups of women crowded around tables, grazing on giant bowls of lettuce and sipping water with lemon wedges.

The hostess led Grace to a table against the window. It had taken her awhile to get used to eating alone in restaurants, but as long as she didn't see anyone she knew, it was okay.

She unfolded her napkin and laid it in her lap.

"Grace?"

Damn. So much for that.

One of the grazers at the table beside hers was leaning so far back in her chair Grace was afraid she'd topple over

25

backward. Motherhood had made her hypersensitive to behaviors apt to result in head injury.

"Grace Poleiski?" the woman said.

"Yes?"

"It's me, Roseanna Janosik, from Chesterfield High."

"Roseanna! Wow, how long has it been?"

"Since the last reunion, I guess. What, eight, nine years?" Roseanna squeezed out of her chair and came to sit at Grace's table. "You look great! What's going on with you?"

"Eh, you know. It's always something."

"I hear that. Hey, what're you doing tonight? Some of the girls are getting together at a club downtown. They'd die if you walked in."

Grace thought about the salmon and new potatoes in her fridge. "All the way to Philly? I don't know…"

"Come on. It's fifteen miles, not the other end of the Earth. Live a little. Leave the kids home with your husband and come out and play. The club is supposed to be a riot. There's a DJ playing all eighties music. It'll be just like high school."

Grace had a sudden flashback to high school. The sausage-curl hair, giant belts, parachute pants. Smoking in the girls' room. Making lip gloss in science lab. She smiled.

She and Roseanna had been good friends. In fact, she'd had a lot of good friends.

Grace's mother had always told her those were the best days of her life, but she'd never believed it.

How was that possible when one strategically placed blemish could put you on the pariah list for a week? When the wrong look from the right guy could annihilate your confidence for a month? When there was no bigger horror than having your period on gym day and having to take a shower in front of twenty other girls?

God, she missed those days.

It was hard to admit, but her mother had been right.

Roseanna squeezed her hand. "So, what do you say? Wanna come?"

"Why not?" Grace said. "Sounds like fun."

"Great." Roseanna scribbled on a napkin. "Here's the address of the club. Meet us there around nine."

Grace pulled her Day-Timer out of her bag and penciled it in and then ordered a salad.

And a margarita. Rocks. No salt.

Friday, 1:30 p.m.
Slow Brenda

"Look at y-o-o-o-u." Misty Hinkle grabbed Grace's hand and pulled her into a living room the size of a hockey rink, and almost as cold. Six card tables were huddled together in the center of the room. Probably for warmth.

"Look at Gra-a-a-a-ace everybody. Doesn't she look fa-a-a-abulous?" The women sitting around the tables

27

tore themselves away from the snacks long enough to glance at her.

"Oh, stop it, Misty," Grace said. "It's just a haircut."

"It's not just a haircut. You went blond." There was an accusatory note in Lorraine's voice.

"I needed a change. What can I say?" Grace caught the knowing glances ricocheting around the room and wondered how long these ladies of modest society would continue to invite her to their functions.

There was currently only one divorced woman in the group, and Grace had a feeling they only kept her around to talk about her behind her back. All the rest of the unfortunately uncoupled had been drummed out of the pack within weeks of their divorces being finalized.

Face it. No one wanted a suddenly single woman running around at one of their holiday parties, talking about how hard it was to get a date when your boobs sagged and your thighs jiggled. Why invite the ghost of Christmas Future?

"I, for one, liked the ponytail," said Brenda McNaull. She pointed to the chair across from hers and motioned for Grace to sit down. "We're partners today."

"Great," Grace said. She should have had a couple more margaritas at lunch. Brenda was the most maddeningly slow card player in the world.

"Pe-e-eople." Misty clapped her hands. "La-a-adies, ple-e-ease. A couple of announcements before we begin."

The room quieted. Slightly.

"Tha-a-an-nk you. Once again, Meredith is looking for volunteers for the Herpes Walk—"

"Hirschsprung's!"

"Sor-r-r-ry—Hirshbaum's Walk. Kathy needs crafts for the Literacy Fair, and Grace is collecting clothes for the Goodwill again today. Leave your bags by the door. And I don't mean the ones under your eyes. *Haw haw!* Oka-a-a-ay, ladies. Let's play!"

Brenda examined the tiny glass dish of nuts at the corner of the card table. "Can you believe this chintzy spread?" She plucked an almond from the dish between two long, manicured fingernails and popped it into her mouth.

"So what's the game today?" Grace asked.

"Pinochle," Brenda said.

The two other women at the table rolled their eyes. It was going to be a long afternoon.

Friday, 4:10 p.m.
Date with Ludmilla

The parking lot at Megan's school was nearly empty. Field hockey wasn't exactly a big draw, as witnessed by the fact that the snack bar wasn't even open.

Grace pulled a couple of grocery bags out of the back of the minivan and looked around. No sign of Tom's car.

Not yet, anyway. But Grace knew he'd be there. He hadn't missed one of Meg's home games since she'd started playing field hockey. Or one of Kevin's soccer matches, or one of Callie's band recitals. Grace had to admit, he was a good father. A lousy husband, but a good father.

Grace picked her way to the field, her high heels aerating the grass. She'd forgotten to bring sneakers.

She plunked the grocery bags down on the bench at the sidelines and unloaded the supplies—a giant plastic bag of quartered oranges, homemade chocolate chip cookies, paper cups and two industrial-sized bottles of Gatorade.

Coach Ludmilla, a hairy but not completely unattractive Hungarian woman, winked at her from the center line. Grace waved.

She wondered if theirs could be considered a monogamous relationship. Did Ludmilla wink exclusively at her, or did she wink at every mother who brought cookies and Gatorade? Maybe they were just dating.

Maybe she needed to get a life.

She watched as Megan dribbled the ball down the field and smacked it toward the goal cage. It hit the post and bounced out of bounds. She saw Megan's gaze search the sidelines. Grace waved, but Megan was looking elsewhere.

Grace looked over her shoulder. Sure enough, Tom stood near the risers, alone. He hesitated before heading toward her.

The official blew the whistle to indicate halftime, and Ludmilla trotted over to the bench.

"Sorry I'm late," Grace said. "My afternoon, uh, appointment ran a little long." *Thank you, Brenda.*

"No problem," Ludmilla said. "Thanks for bringing the snacks again, Grace."

"Sure. The team's looking good."

"You bet." Ludmilla sidled next to her. "We're looking for an assistant coach. Someone to carry equipment and keep the stats. You interested?"

"Sorry," Grace said, handing the coach a cup of Gatorade. "I've got too much on my plate right now. Maybe next year."

Ludmilla looked disappointed. "Sure. Well, I've got to get these ladies ready for the second half. Will you pour some drinks for the team?"

"Of course."

While Grace bent over a row of paper cups, she saw Tom's three-hundred-dollar shoes approach. Unfortunately, he was in them.

"Grace, how are you?"

She continued pouring. "Same as this morning."

"Have you thought about what I asked you?"

"You mean how you want me to perform an illegal act that might get me arrested and destroy our children's lives in order to get what I deserve out of this marriage anyway?"

He sighed. "I'm not trying to screw you."

"Really?" She straightened. "Well that's a relief, because I'm pretty sure you got the K-Y in the settlement."

They both clammed up as the girls filed past the bench, inhaling oranges and cookies and Gatorade. In seconds they were gone, leaving nothing but empty plates and crushed cups in their wake.

Tom stuffed his hands in his pockets. "You don't know what's going on, Grace. You don't know what my life is like. I just want—"

"I'm not really interested in what you want, Tom. At this moment, I'm just trying to be here for one of my kids. I hope we can be civil for their sakes, but as far as your wants and needs—well, I guess that's what you've got Marlene for."

Tom's jaw twitched.

Grace wondered if he and Marlene were having problems. So, why should she give a damn? She had her own relationships to worry about.

Ludmilla waved to her from across the field.

Okay. So maybe it was time to reconsider her definition of *relationship*.

She looked over at Megan, chatting with her friends,

watching her and Tom out of the corner of her eye. She'd been through so much the past year. They all had.

She didn't want to put the kids through a move, on top of everything else.

"Alright," she said, forcing a smile for Megan's benefit. "I'll do it."

"Oh, God. That's great, Gracie. I knew I could count on you." He pulled an envelope from his jacket pocket.

"You brought them *with you?*"

He gave her a sheepish grin. "Just in case."

She looked around nervously, expecting the cops to be waiting for her just outside the fence. But there was no one there.

The game had resumed, and Ludmilla and the team moved to the far end of the field, leaving her and Tom pretty much alone. She spread the papers out on the bench, studying the signature he wanted her to forge.

"Roger Davis," she read. "Isn't that your boss?"

He nodded but didn't offer any more information. And she didn't ask.

She had the feeling she wasn't signing an authorization for an extra day of vacation, but she figured the less she knew about all of this, the better.

"I'll have to practice the signature a few times before I sign them. I'll get them back to you."

"When?"

She pulled her Day-Timer out of her purse and flipped through it.

"Will Marlene be home tomorrow morning?"

"No, I don't think so."

"Good. I'll bring them over then." She shoved the papers back into the envelope and stuck them in her purse. "The kids will be at my Mom's this weekend if you want to get in touch with them," she said. "Kevin has a soccer game tomorrow."

"I know," Tom said. "I'll be there."

"How about if we also meet at the notary office Tuesday morning?" she said. "You can bring the papers for the house, and the title to the 'Vette, too."

He gave her a sickly smile.

"Don't worry," she said. "It'll be relatively painless. We'll get it all over with at once. Like pulling off a Band-Aid."

He opened his mouth as if he might say something, but he didn't. He just walked back toward the bleachers, hands in his pockets, his three-hundred-dollar shoes sucking mud.

CHAPTER 2.5

Friday, 5:58 p.m.
Roadkill

The asshole drove right past their meeting place.

According to the plan, as soon as Balboa arrived in Philly, he was supposed to drive straight to the gym and call from a pay phone. Shit. He was gonna screw them.

Pete had followed Balboa's rented green Taurus all the way from the airport. Balboa's own car, a cherry 1959 Buick, still sat in the VIP parking lot at the airport.

If Pete hadn't suspected Balboa was turning on them and staked out the baggage claim, he'd never even have known the guy was back in town a day early.

He flipped open his cell phone. "Lou. He's back."

"No shit."

"I followed him from the airport. He just passed the

gym. I need you to go wait at his house. I doubt he'll show up there, but you never know."

"Right. I'm on it."

Pete snapped the phone closed.

In front of him, the Taurus eased into the exit lane. It looked like Balboa was heading for City Avenue.

Pete jockeyed through four lanes of frantic expressway traffic but just missed the exit.

Damn.

When Pete caught up to him, that son of a bitch Nick Balboa was dead meat.

CHAPTER 3

Friday, 7:12 p.m.
Oh, Mother!

As she drove toward her childhood home in Ambler, Grace felt younger and younger until, by the time she pulled into her parents' driveway, she was eight again.

In her mind she could hear the sprinklers whirring, and smell the newly cut grass of her youth. She looked across the street, half expecting to see her best friend, Sherri Rasmussen, playing hopscotch on the sidewalk.

"Okay, guys, everybody out of the car. Callie, don't forget your flute."

As the kids dragged their crap up the sidewalk, the door opened and Grace's mother stuck her head out. "My babies are here! Andrew, the children are here! Come help them with their things."

"Hi, Mom." Grace herded the kids into the house and bussed her mother on the cheek. "Thanks for taking them this weekend."

"Well, your father and I can imagine how difficult things must be for you, with the—" she stuck her head out the door and scanned the neighborhood for spies "—*divorce*."

Divorce was one of the words in Grace's mother's vocabulary fit only for whispering.

"You can say it out loud, Mom. It's not a dirty word."

Her mother pulled a face. "Come on in."

"Actually, I was kind of in a hurry."

"So you don't have time for a soda? Come in for a minute. I want to show you something."

Grace sighed. She knew once she got sucked over the threshold, it would be at least a half an hour before she got out of there.

The kids thumped up the stairs, already arguing about who'd get to play her father's Nintendo first. Grace followed her mother to the kitchen and sat on one of the vinyl-covered chairs. They were the same chairs she'd sat on as a child, once sadly out of style but suddenly retro chic.

"Look what I made in craft class," her mother said. She held out a tissue box cover constructed of yarn-covered plastic mesh. God Bless You was cross-stitched into the side in block letters.

"Nice."

"Here, take it. I made it for you. And you know, you can come with me next week. We're making birds out of Styrofoam."

"That's nice, but I can't."

Her mother took a diet soda from the refrigerator. "Why not? Now that Tom is gone, what are you doing with your time?"

Grace got up to get a glass from the cupboard. "I've got plenty to do, Mom."

"Like what?"

"Well, tonight I'm meeting some of my old high school friends for a drink downtown."

Her mother's eyebrows shot up and disappeared beneath her heavily hair-sprayed bangs. "Really? Do I know them?"

Déjà vu. How many times had Grace seen that look growing up? She felt inexplicably guilty, and she hadn't even lied about anything. Yet.

"Roseanna Janosik's going to be there. I ran into her today at Beruglia's."

Her mother sat down at the table. "Roseanna Janosik. Isn't that the girl who got caught smoking at cheerleading camp?" She pulled a face.

"That was Cecilia Stavros. And Jesus, Mom. That was a hundred years ago."

"You're right, of course. People change. Look at you."

"What's that supposed to mean?"

Her mother shrugged. "So who was Roseanna Janosik?" She tapped her chin. "I remember! She was the one who was crazy about that band and followed them everywhere."

"Right. Mullet."

"What? What's a mullet?"

"A bad haircut. And the name of the band Roseanna followed." Grace chugged her soda. "C'mon, tell me. What did you mean I've changed?"

Her mother got up from the table and took Grace's empty glass. "Oh, for heaven's sake, Grace, I didn't mean anything by it. Is that what you're wearing?"

"As a matter of fact, it is." Grace tugged the hem of her black skirt, but it refused to budge. She buttoned the red Chinese silk jacket Tom had given her the Valentine's Day before last. It had been the only thing in her closet remotely resembling club attire.

Her mother raised her eyebrows again. "Well, have fun. Tell Roseanna I said hello."

"Right."

Grace stalked to the bottom of the stairs. "Megan, Callie, Kevin. I'm leaving now!"

Megan and Kevin shouted a muffled goodbye. Callie stuck her head over the second-floor railing. "Bye, Mom. Have fun without us."

Grace tamped down a sudden attack of guilt. "I'll miss you."

"I'll miss you, too. Can we make brownies when I come home?" Callie could sense Grace's subtle vibrations of guilt like a fine-tuned seismograph.

"Sure."

"Grace, are you still here?" her mother called from the kitchen.

If she didn't get out of there soon, her mother would be dragging her up to the guest bathroom to show her the decorative fertility mask she'd made out of half of a bleach bottle.

Grace wiggled her fingers at Callie and slipped out the front door.

Friday, 8:08 p.m.
Killing Me Softly

Grace sped down the Blue Route in the eight-year-old BMW that used to be Tom's but was now hers. He'd insisted on getting a manual transmission, and now she was stuck with it—a real pain in the butt while she was trying to wipe noses and juggle juice boxes.

She much preferred the minivan, but she'd be damned if she was going to pull into a club driving the family taxi.

She fiddled with the radio. Why were all the stations in her car set to soft rock? When, exactly, had her eardrums surrendered?

41

She searched the dial for the station that played all eighties, all the time. AC/DC's "You Shook Me All Night Long" came on and she smiled. It took her back to when she and her girlfriends would cruise the back roads in an old Dodge Dart looking for keg parties, blasting this song and singing at the top of their lungs.

How sad. Somehow she'd gone from AC/DC to Celine Dion. From keg parties to the occasional glass of chardonnay. Was that what her mother meant? Was that how she'd changed?

She knew it was that, and a whole lot more. She used to have spirit. She used to take risks.

But when she'd married Tom, somehow it had been easy to accept the security and stability he provided in exchange for a few little changes. Higher necklines. Lower hemlines. The Junior League instead of her bowling league.

She drove around for almost an hour, reprogramming the buttons on her radio and thinking about all the crazy things she used to do, forcing herself not to worry that she was going to be late.

Eventually, she pulled into the parking lot of the club. She squinted up at the sign.

Caligula?

She checked the address in her Day-Timer. Sure enough, it was right.

She almost backed out of the lot, but images of her closet filled with navy poly-blend slacks and V-neck sweaters bolstered her nerve.

She could be every bit as crazy as her teenage alter ego. She *could*.

She got out of the car and tugged her skirt down as far as she could.

"Bring on the Romans," she said to the dark.

Friday, 9:13 p.m.
Flaming Togas

"ID, please."

The guy at the door wore baggy jeans and a black T-shirt with a picture of a snarling bulldog. His fingers worked the buttons of a Game Boy with lightning speed.

The B-52's "Love Shack" blasted out through the open door of the club.

Grace leaned in so the bouncer could hear her over the noise. "You're kidding me, right? Have you even *looked* at me? I was twenty-one when this song actually came out."

He shined a flashlight in her face. "Sorry 'bout that. Five bucks."

He stepped aside, and she walked straight into ancient Rome. Or a Hollywood-meets-Las Vegas version of it, anyway.

Buff, gorgeous, toga-clad waiters and waitresses wandered the faux-marble floor carrying trays of colorful drinks. Buff, gorgeous, denim-clad patrons sipped them while leaning against faux-marble columns. They were all so young. Well, most of them, anyway.

Grace had no trouble spotting her old high school friends. They were the only ones not trying to look bored.

Roseanna must have had one eye on the door, because she waved to Grace as soon as she walked in.

"Oh. My. God. It's Grace Poleiski," somebody shrieked.

Grace smiled. "Hi, everybody."

The women at the table jumped up and swarmed around her. She exchanged a quick hug with each of them, blinking back the tears that had inexplicably formed in her eyes.

"Sit," commanded Roseanna. "We just ordered a round of Flaming Togas."

Grace hooked her handbag over the back of a chair and sat down, taking in all the changes in her friends. "Cecilia, you look great. You lost weight?"

"Forty pounds. Ephedra, until they took it off the market. If I hadn't started smoking again to compensate, I'd probably look like the Michelin Man already. Hey, you're looking good, too, Grace."

"Yeah? I guess you could say I lost some weight, too. About two hundred pounds."

"What! How'd you do that?"

"It just walked away."

It took the girls a minute to figure out what she was talking about.

"Your husband," Roseanna said.

Grace nodded.

Cecilia shook her head. "No shit. When did that happen?"

"January second. Screwing me over was his New Year's resolution, I guess."

A waiter arrived with a tray of pale orange shots and set one in front of each woman. He pulled a pack of matches out of the folds of his toga and lit the shots. Low blue flames danced on the surface of the liquor.

"Don't forget to blow 'em out before you drink 'em," he said. "We've had a couple of mishaps."

Roseanna smiled. "Remember when Dannie accidentally lit her hair on fire while she was smoking a cigarette in the girls' bathroom?"

"What did she expect?" said Cecilia. "She used so much hair spray, her hair wouldn't have moved in a hurricane."

"Come on," Dannie said. "My hair wasn't any worse than anyone else's. In fact, I remember Grace getting hers tangled in the volleyball net in gym class. It had to be at least a foot high."

They all laughed.

Grace ordered a margarita and another round of shots.

The waiter walked away, his tight little butt all but peeking out from under the toga.

Dannie propped her chin up on her hand. "Those look like my sheets he's wearing."

"You wish," Cecilia said.

Grace pulled a bunch of pictures out of her purse and passed them to Roseanna.

She'd found them in a shoebox along with the dance card and tiny pencil from her prom, a football homecoming program and the hunk of yarn she'd used to wrap around her high school boyfriend's class ring.

"Oh, God. I remember this skirt," Roseanna said. "I couldn't get one thigh in there, now."

"Sure you could," Dannie said. "It would be a little tight, though."

"Ha-ha." Roseanna passed the pictures to Cecilia. "Hey, remember when we used to play truth or dare in study hall?"

"Yeah. I think Mr. Montrose almost had a heart attack," said Cecilia. "You'd always dare me to lean over his desk to ask him a question."

"He couldn't stand up for the rest of the class."

"To Mr. Montrose," said Grace, raising the shot the waiter had just delivered. They all toasted Mr. Montrose and blew out their Flaming Togas.

"Let's play," said Roseanna.

"Play what?"

"Truth or dare."

"Here?" Grace said. "You're crazy."

"It'll be fun," said Dannie.

"Why not?" said Cecilia.

Music thumped in the background. Mötley Crüe belted out "Girls, Girls, Girls."

"What the hell," Grace said.

Saturday, 11:44 p.m.
Gracie's Secret

Grace was drunk.

Not merely drunk but what they once affectionately called shit faced.

Roseanna's head rested on the table, surrounded by empty shot glasses. Dannie balanced a straw on her nose. Cecilia puffed on a cigarette, making tiny smoke rings by tapping on her cheek.

Grace had quit smoking soon after she'd married Tom. He disapproved of the habit. Said it made her look cheap. Unlike Marlene, who looked so classy covered in grape jelly.

"Gimme one of those," Grace said.

Cecilia rolled a cigarette across the table. "Okay. Grace's turn. Truth or dare?"

47

"Truth."

"What's the worst thing you've ever done? And high school shenanigans don't count."

Grace shook her head. "Nothing. I've never done anything remotely bad."

"Oh, come *on*," Dannie said, taking the straw off her nose. "We know you better than that."

"Seriously. I'm the perfect wife. The perfect mother. The perfect daughter. The worst thing I've ever done is wear this skirt, which is definitely too short for me. Gimme a light."

"Dare it is, then," Roseanna said, dragging herself to a sitting position.

"What? I told you—"

"No way. You're lying," said Cecilia. "But that's okay, because I have the perfect dare for you."

Grace raised her eyebrows.

"Go over there and give your underwear—" Cecilia pointed toward the bar "—to him."

Grace sucked in her cheeks.

The guy looked as if he'd stepped off the pages of GQ. Black turtleneck. Black leather jacket. Dark, brooding eyes. He sat in a pool of light shining down from the ceiling as if he were some sort of fallen angel. The most gorgeous in-the-flesh man she'd ever seen.

Gorgeous, and young.

"Nun-uh. He's a baby," Grace said.

"All you gotta do is give him your undies, Grace. It's not like you've never given a guy your undies before, right?" Dannie's smile was evil. Evil and smug.

Grace wobbled to her feet. Damn. He might be young, but she wasn't *that* old. She still had decent legs and a not-so-bad ass. "Fine. Consider it done."

She marched to the ladies' room, only to find a line a mile long. While she waited, she had plenty of time to reconsider her decision. There was something slightly sinister about that man.

She could always go back to the table and make up a story for the "truth" portion of the game. Surely she could come up with something suitably shocking.

Grace looked over at her friends, who watched her with a mixture of admiration and disbelief. No. She couldn't lie to them. Way back when, they'd all sworn on their posters of Jon Bon Jovi. No lying at truth or dare. It was a matter of honor.

But there's no way I'm telling them the truth.

Her own parents didn't know about her arrest, and she intended to keep it that way. It had been a youthful indiscretion, and now that she was a hair past youthful, there was absolutely no need to be indiscreet. Especially since she just did it again—and this time, she definitely knew better.

So?

So she'd take the dare and go give GQ her underpants.

She slipped into the bathroom and balanced against the toilet paper holder as she stripped off her underpants, happy that she'd worn a decent pair without holes. Sometimes following motherly advice paid off at the oddest moments.

Stuffing the panties deep into her pocket, she fought her way out of the bathroom and through the crowd that had suddenly grown up around the bar. She tried not to look obvious as she slid in next to the Roman god, elbowing a pouty waif off of the bar stool beside him. The girl attempted a threatening look.

Grace laughed. "Please. I've shaved parmesan thicker than you. Get going."

The girl slinked away to a group of equally emaciated friends.

Grace ordered a margarita from the bartender, took the cigarette Cecilia had given her out of her pocket and stuck it between her lips.

"Excuse me, do you have a light?"

Adonis smiled, his teeth shining like Chiclets in the bluish light. "Sure."

He pulled a lighter out of his pocket and sparked it, holding the flame out in front of her. "How you doin', sweetheart?" He pronounced it "sweethawt" in a perfect South Philly accent.

She leaned in and sucked the flames into the cigarette,

drawing the smoke deep in her lungs. It wasn't at all as pleasant as she remembered.

"Just a minute," she rasped, holding up a finger while she hacked into her palm. And into her sleeve. And into the hair of the girl next to her.

GQ handed her the margarita and she sucked down half of it.

"Grace."

"What?" he said. He looked confused.

"My name. It's Grace."

"Yeah. I'm Nick. Nick Balboa." He affected a slur and shadowboxed the air. "Youse know, like Rocky?"

"Right. Were you even born when that movie came out?"

"Almost."

She grinned, aware that she probably looked incredibly dopey but for some reason was unable to stop.

Now what?

She decided that since this was a game of truth or dare, she'd just tell him the truth.

"Nick."

"Yeah?"

Damn, he was good-looking. The dimple on his chin momentarily distracted her.

"Nick, I have a confession. Do you see those women over there?" She pointed to her friends. They all stared back like they were watching a bad reality TV show. All except Roseanna, whose head was back on the table.

Nick nodded.

"They dared me to come over here and give you something."

Nick grinned. "Like what?"

"Like my underwear."

He didn't look the slightest bit surprised. She guessed women offered him their underwear on a pretty regular basis, much as they did Tom Jones.

"I have to give you my underwear," she continued, "in order to satisfy some sick need they have to humiliate me."

He shrugged. "Okay."

She sidled closer, and dangled her panties in front of him so the girls could see.

Nick gave her panties an appraising look. He crumpled them up and stuck them in his pocket. Then he grabbed her around the waist and pulled her close. "Wanna give your friends something better to watch?"

Oh, my.

"Like what?"

"Like this." He leaned in close, and she shut her eyes. He smelled of leather, Aramis and tequila, three of her favorite things. She knew what was coming, but she was afraid if she looked she'd chicken out. And she really didn't want to chicken out.

The DJ was playing the Cure's "Just Like Heaven," and the beat reverberated through the bar beneath her elbow. Nick's lips were mere inches away.

What was it the Romans used to say?

Oh, yeah. *Carpe diem.*

Saturday, 12:17 a.m.
Goodbye Girls

When they finally came up for air—about thirteen minutes later—Cecilia was standing behind them.

"You okay?" she asked.

Grace nodded.

"How are you getting home?"

"I'll call a cab."

"Okay." Cecilia winked at Nick. "Nice to meet you."

"Likewise," he said. Rose Frost lipstick smeared his lips.

Cecilia returned to the table and waved to Grace. She made a fist and held it to her cheek like a telephone receiver, mouthing the words, "Call me." Then she and Dannie slung their arms around Roseanna and dragged her through the crowd toward the door.

"Your friends leaving?" Nick asked.

"Apparently."

For a split second Grace thought maybe she should leave with them, but when she tried to stand up, the room spun.

53

Nick kissed her again, stroking her arms with his palms. It was like kissing Vinnie Barbarino, Scott Baio and Rob Lowe, all rolled into one. Just a teeny bit surreal.

Nick slid his hand down to hers and linked her fingers in his and—

Stopped.

He stopped kissing her.

He brought her left hand up between them and looked at her fingers.

The diamond band Tom had given her for their tenth anniversary refracted the spotlight above them like a disco ball.

"Nice ring. You married?" Nick asked.

Damn. Why had she worn it?

Oh, yeah. To discourage this very thing. After all, she was a sensible lady. A mother. A woman who wasn't quite divorced. She shouldn't be picking up strange men in bars.

The momentary wave of guilt she felt was quickly replaced by drunken defiance.

She slid the ring off her finger and dropped it into Nick's drink. "Not anymore. Now kiss me."

CHAPTER 3.5

Saturday, 12:49 a.m.
Lady in Red

Who was the babe?

Pete watched Balboa with the blonde in the red jacket for almost twenty minutes. He'd never seen her before, but that didn't mean anything. Balboa always had a roll of cash in his pocket and a girl on his arm. Often, both appeared from nowhere.

Problem was, this one didn't quite look like Balboa's type. His recipe for the perfect woman was forty-five percent silicone, forty-five percent collagen and ten percent ink.

This one, while the clothes she wore weren't exactly conservative, they didn't come close to some of the anti-apparel he'd seen before. Her breasts actually looked real, too, and she didn't have one visible tattoo.

Something was up.

As time went on, the crowd at the bar began to thin. Pete moved to a spot behind Balboa and the female. The woman stood to flag down the bartender, and Pete watched as Balboa's hand cupped her rather spectacular ass.

Life could be so unfair.

Pete ordered another club soda from the waitress and leaned against a column.

If he had to guess, he'd say that Balboa had the memory key on him. According to Pete's sources, Balboa had come straight here after meeting with the Russian's competition, Johnny Iatesta, in Trenton. The asshole. Two years of wheeling and dealing, and the guy was going to screw him? No way.

All Pete had to do was stick close until the horny couple left the club.

He yawned. When in the hell were these two going to get a room?

Just then Balboa slipped something into the pocket of the woman's red jacket. Drugs? Money?

The memory key.

Balboa whispered something in her ear, and they sucked face for another five minutes before she broke away.

She headed straight for Pete, brushing his arm with her breasts as she squeezed by him on her way to the can.

She smelled fantastic. He thought she might have a pretty face, too, but it was dark and he'd been distracted by the rest of her.

He watched the ladies' room, looking forward to her return trip.

She emerged from the bathroom, but instead of coming back toward him she headed for the door.

Pete hustled after her, pushing through the ranks of ultrahip boys and girls pretending not to notice each other. He'd almost reached the door when a guy resembling a woolly mammoth in a tuxedo plowed in.

"'Scuse me."

"No problem." Pete tried to get around him, only to discover six more just like him pouring through the door. Seven equally large women in ruffled bridesmaid gowns followed close behind the men.

Pete got caught in the undertow and was pulled back into the club, surfing a wave of Aqua Velva and powder-blue taffeta. Somehow he managed to squeeze through the wedding party and reached the door just in time to see a cab pull away from the curb.

Pete smacked the door with the palm of his hand.

Now what?

He turned and went back into the club. No way was he going to let Balboa disappear.

But by the time he fought his way back into the bar,

the only thing left sitting at Balboa's bar stool was a lip-stick-smudged margarita glass and an ashtray full of butts.

"Shit," Pete muttered.

It really wasn't his day.

CHAPTER 4

Saturday, 7:54 a.m.
Turning Japanese

Someone was sticking needles into her eyes. Not sewing needles, but long, thick hypodermics.

Wait. What was that? The smoke detector? The kids!

Grace leaped out of bed and ran for the door, slipping on the silk jacket that lay on the floor, smacking her head on the ceramic cat at the end of the bed.

She lay on her back, staring up at the frosted glass light fixture on the ceiling.

That noise wasn't the smoke detector going off. It was her alarm clock.

"Crap." She winced at the sound of her own voice.

She rolled onto her stomach and pushed up onto all fours. Just the thought of standing left her weak with nausea.

She crawled into the bathroom on her hands and knees and laid her cheek on the cool Japanese porcelain tile floor. Her tongue felt like one of Kevin's gym socks and, she imagined, smelled like it, too.

What have I done to myself?

Her hand bore an ugly blue ink blot—the stamp for the club. And on her palm she'd written a number—1767.

1767? What the hell was that?

A high, wavering voice echoed in her head. "In 1767, the Townshend Acts were implemented by the British on the American colonies…" It was Mrs. Dietz, her ninth-grade American History teacher.

Grace squinted at the numbers again. Why in the hell would she have written the date of the Townshend Acts on her hand?

She debated taking a shower but imagined the water would probably feel like Niagara Falls beating down on her head. She managed to pull on a sweat suit and comb her new pain-in-the-ass haircut without throwing up.

She took three aspirins and staggered downstairs to check her Day-Timer.

Meals on Wheels, the Goodwill drop and then Tom's.

She'd signed the papers he'd given her. No, she'd *forged* the papers (why not call a spade a spade?), and she just wanted to get rid of them and get on with her life.

Crap.

She dragged a giant green trash bag full of clothes from her closet. In a moment of pique over the bump on her head and her prick of an ex-husband, she stuffed the red silk jacket into the bag.

Saturday, 9:11 a.m.
Mrs. Beeber and Mr. Pickles

"Who is it?" Mrs. Beeber peered at Grace through the smeary film coating the window of the storm door. Her head resembled a small dried apple nestled atop the collar of her purple turtleneck.

"Meals on Wheels, Mrs. Beeber."

"I didn't think you were coming today. You're late."

"I'm not late, Mrs. Beeber. Will you open the door?"

Mrs. Beeber squinted at her watch, and shook her head. "You're eleven minutes late."

One cup of instant coffee—made with hot tap water and consumed while standing over the sink—had not prepared Grace for this day. She took three calming breaths. *Nadi shodhana.* Her yoga instructor would be proud.

"I'm very sorry, Mrs. Beeber. I couldn't find my car keys."

In fact, she hadn't been able to find her purse. She'd scoured the whole house, with no luck. She must have left it at the club.

She'd allowed herself a few minutes of heart-thumping panic. Her cell phone was in there, along with her car keys and house keys (which explained why the panty hose she'd worn last night had been covered with mulch, and the spare key she hid under a rock in the flower bed was now on the table near the back door).

But, worst of all, the papers she was supposed to return to Tom that morning were in that purse.

When she went out to the garage, she realized she had to go back to Caligula anyway, to pick up her car. Surely her purse would be there, safe and snug in the arms of the Game Boy–playing bouncer.

She'd chosen to ignore all logic to the contrary. Her stomach just couldn't take it.

So she'd snagged her spare keys from the hook by the door, and took the minivan for her morning appointments.

"Helloooo?" Mrs. Beeber called her back to Earth, and made a sour face. "Are you coming in with that?"

She held the screen door open and Grace entered, bearing a white tray covered with plastic wrap she'd picked up on her way there.

Mrs. Beeber squinted at the tray. "Is it a kosher meal?"

Grace bit the inside of her cheek. "You aren't Jewish, Mrs. Beeber."

"Yeah, but they give you more with them kosher meals."

Grace set the tray on Mrs. Beeber's mutton-gray

Formica countertop. "I'm pretty sure everyone gets the same amount, whether it's kosher or not. Is everything okay with you?"

"As a matter of fact, my sciatica's a bitch and my son never calls me."

"I'm sorry to hear that."

"And I got the runs from that ham casserole you brought the other day."

"I didn't bring you a ham casserole."

"You didn't?"

"No."

Mrs. Beeber scratched her chin. "Now wait, I remember. It wasn't you. It was my neighbor, Peggy. I should know better than to eat anything she gives me. One time, oh, I guess it was nineteen-seventy-eight or nine…I remember I was watching *Dallas*…she brought me this disgusting meat loaf—"

"Mrs. Beeber, I really have to get going. I have three more meals to deliver."

"Oh. Well. Can you help me with something before you leave?"

"You know I'm not supposed to…"

"But it isn't for me. It's for Mr. Pickles."

Mr. Pickles was Mrs. Beeber's cat, a giant old Persian with male pattern baldness and a lazy eye, who'd hissed at Grace on more than one occasion. Not a huge motivator.

"Please?" Mrs. Beeber's wizened face sank deeper into the turtleneck sweater.

Grace sighed. "Okay. What do you need?"

Saturday, 10:41 a.m.
Shake It Up

"Rough night, eh?"

"Will you just help me, please?" Grace struggled under the weight of the bag filled with clothes, her arms weak from hefting a fifty-pound bag of cat food up forty stairs from Mrs. Beeber's cellar.

Grace doubted Mr. Pickles would live long enough to see the food at the bottom of that bag.

Martha Moradjiewski, the clerk at the Goodwill, grabbed one side of the garbage bag and helped Grace drag it across the floor to the counter.

"You look hungover," the clerk said.

"Just a little."

"Try a vanilla milkshake. They always help me."

Grace imagined Martha drank a lot of milkshakes, what with having a couple of sons who spent the day sniffing nail polish, a live-in mother-in-law with Alzheimer's and a husband who considered pot a major food group.

Grace slid her sunglasses on. "I'll give it a shot."

Six minutes later she pulled out of McDonald's, shake in hand, heading for home. She took a sip, her eyeballs nearly imploding from the suction necessary to draw a mouthful of the stuff.

"Ugh."

She stuck the shake in a cup holder and rolled down the window, trying to clear her head. *What* happened last night?

There were togas, of course. And cigarettes. And primo butts.

She remembered shots. Lots of shots. And lots of margaritas, too.

She remembered talking about movies and music and high school haircuts. And boys. And men.

Beyond that, nothing.

She pulled into her driveway, not too sick to admire the bright red Japanese maple near the front door. She couldn't imagine not seeing that maple every day.

What she'd done in order to keep it crept back into her consciousness. One small act of forgery, and the landscaping was forever hers.

She gagged and shoved a fist into her mouth to keep from barfing into the bushes.

Hey, at least they were *her* bushes. Right?

Saturday, 11:39 a.m.
Lord of the Ring

After the needles in her eyes had been replaced by tiny straight pins and there was absolutely nothing left in her stomach to puke up, Grace made a pot of coffee and braved the thirty seconds of blinding sunlight to fetch the paper from the lawn.

She needed a few minutes to get herself together before she called a cab and went back down to the city for her car.

She sat down with her World's Best Mom mug and opened the obituaries, half expecting to see her own name, when she stopped short.

Her anniversary band.

The twenty-thousand-dollar diamond and sapphire Tiffany anniversary band.

It wasn't shooting spectacular prisms of light across the kitchen ceiling. Nor was it catching on the edge of the paper like it always did or digging uncomfortably into the sides of her fingers.

It wasn't there.

She took the stairs two at a time, ignoring the persistent sensation that her head was going to explode.

The crystal dish on her dresser where she usually kept the ring was empty. Beside it lay a red credit card.

No, not a credit card. A hotel room key.

"Jesus." She clutched her head between her palms. The previous night played in her head like a Fellini film.

The last time she had seen her ring, it was lighting up that gorgeous guy's smile. He'd chugged the drink she'd put it in, and caught it in his teeth, like a frat boy playing quarters.

Her stomach churned. Oh, God. What was his name? Nick something. Barlow? Bartlett?

No, something more ethnic.

She squeezed her eyes shut.

Balboa. Like Rocky. Yo, Adrian. That was it!

It all came back to her in a rush. He was staying at the Baccus, a swanky hotel in Center City. He'd invited her back there. But she'd chickened out. Took a powder. Scrammed. Punked out.

Why is the voice in my head talking like Sam Spade?

She took a moment to hyperventilate before she grabbed the room key from the dresser.

Okay. Alright.

Just what were the odds a young, gorgeous godlike stud would still be there, waiting for her to show up, with a twenty-thousand-dollar ring between his teeth?

She ran into the bathroom and ralphed in the sink.

CHAPTER 4.5

Saturday, 11:53 a.m.
Over Easy

It had taken Pete all night, but he'd finally tracked Balboa down at the Baccus. Dumb shit had checked in using a fake name but his own credit card.

Pete stepped into the elevator and flipped open his cell phone.

"Lou. I'm at the Baccus. Any movement from the Russian?"

"Nah. Everything's quiet here. Just the girlfriend coming and going. You shoulda seen what she was wearing last night." Lou whistled into the phone.

"Glad to hear you're having a good time."

"Hey, a man's gotta entertain himself."

"Just make sure you're not 'entertaining' yourself when the Russian makes a move."

Lou laughed, and Pete flipped the phone closed.

The elevator arrived on the seventeenth floor, and Pete unbuttoned his coat, to give himself easy access to the weapon in his shoulder holster. He didn't think he would need it. Balboa was a lover, not a fighter. But you never knew.

He walked quickly to Balboa's door and waited there, listening. He didn't hear anything, but that wasn't surprising. Balboa typically slept until noon.

He pounded on the door, watching the peephole for light or movement. Still, nothing.

After a cursory look up and down the hall, he pulled a key card from his pocket. The card had been doctored with copper tape, to which he'd attached a wire with a toggle switch hooked to a nine-volt battery. He slid the card into the lock and flipped the switch, holding his breath.

The lock popped, and he pushed the door open.

The room was dark, the curtains still drawn. He flipped the light switch, half expecting to see Balboa snoring in the king-size bed, but he wasn't.

The room was empty.

"Shit."

Pete gave a thorough search through the drawers and the pockets of the clothes hanging in the closet.

He found a pair of pink ladies' underwear and a black

handbag which, a search revealed, belonged to one Grace Becker.

The lady in red.

She had darker hair in the picture on her driver's license, and longer, too. But it was definitely the same broad.

He checked her birth date, and whistled through his teeth. Thirty-seven.

Really not Balboa's type.

But he had to admit, she looked good for her age. Hell, she looked good for any age. Maybe Balboa's taste was improving.

He looked through the handbag again, searching for the memory key, but it wasn't there.

Maybe they'd taken it somewhere. To the Russian or someone else. Iatesta, maybe.

That memory key was worth double what the Russian had agreed to pay for it, and Balboa knew it. He wasn't a stupid guy.

Maybe, if Pete was lucky, Balboa and the lady had just gone to breakfast.

Pete's stomach growled. He should have stopped for something to eat before coming up. A nice plate of eggs and scrapple at the Melrose, or a tall stack of pancakes. Jeez, he could be waiting there all day.

He called Lou again. "Hey, I need you to have

someone checked out for me. A Grace Becker." He read the driver's license number and address.

"Right, boss. By the way, the Russian's girlfriend just left again. She was wearing this stretchy blue skirt, like a tie-dyed thing, with these really high heels..."

Pete sighed, suddenly jealous of Lou, with Skobelov's girlfriend coming and going in her crazy stripper outfits. At least Lou had something to look at.

Pete hung up the phone, turned off the lights and flipped on the TV, turning the volume all the way down and hoping he wouldn't have to wait too long.

CHAPTER 5

Saturday, 12:41 p.m.
Looking for Mr. Goodbody

It didn't hit her until she was in the elevator at the Baccus Hotel, on her way up to the seventeenth floor, that maybe she should have brought some protection. But what kind?

Mace? Condoms?

Both?

Well, it was too late. If she turned around now, she'd never work up the nerve to come back. Besides, the irresistible combination of bad breath, bloodshot eyes and the baggy yoga pants she wore all but guaranteed Mr. Hottie wouldn't come within six feet of her.

Her Lady Keds were silent on the thick, burgundy carpeting of the hall. What in the hell was she going to say to this man?

Hi. Remember me? I'm the slut who gave you my under-wear and played tongue aerobics with you for several hours last night. I'd like my anniversary ring back, please. And as long as I'm here, you wanna make out?

When she arrived at room 1767—she'd finally figured out what the numbers on her palm were—she stopped and took a deep breath. Blood rushed to her head, and she had to squat down for a minute until it rushed back to all the other places it was needed.

She was never going to drink again. Ever.

She tapped lightly on the door. No answer.

Maybe he was still sleeping. Or maybe he'd picked up another woman at the bar. Probably the see-through nymphet who'd been sitting next to him when she'd first approached. Or maybe one of the toga-clad waitresses.

Or waiters.

She started to hyperventilate. Oh, God. She didn't know anything about this man. He'd probably already pawned her ring and spent the money on crack, or heroin or the ponies.

What? Was she living in an HBO documentary now? *Jesus.*

She forced herself to breathe and knocked again.

Nothing.

What if he'd already checked out? She rooted through her pockets, producing the key card he'd slipped her.

Saying a tiny prayer to the patron saint of Those with Poor Judgment, she slipped the key card into the handle.

The green light lit up.

She pushed the handle down, and, with an obnoxiously loud clack, the door swung open.

"Hello? Nick?"

The curtains were drawn shut, and the room was dark.

"Nick?" She stepped into the room.

The bathroom was immediately to her left. She turned on the light. A shaving kit stood open on the counter, next to the sink. The air was damp and smelled of Aramis. She closed her eyes and breathed it in.

Across from the bathroom, the mirrored closet door was pushed open. Inside hung the pants and shirt Nick had worn at the bar. The leather jacket was missing.

She checked the pockets of the pants and shirt. No ring.

She wandered into the room and turned on the lamp on top of the dresser. The surface was littered with crumpled receipts, soda cans and empty potato chip bags.

Jeez. How did men do it? They could eat crap like this and not gain an ounce. Life was so unfair.

Going against every natural instinct, she resisted the urge to clean up the mess. Instead, she poked through it with the hotel ballpoint.

Like he'd leave a twenty-thousand-dollar diamond ring under a candy wrapper. Right.

Feeling an overwhelming urge to pee, she reached for the top drawer of the dresser. Before she could open it, she caught a movement in the dresser mirror.

She spun around. "Who are you?"

A man in a trench coat sat up against the headboard, his long legs stretched out over the bedspread and crossed at the ankles.

If Nick was GQ, this guy was Sears and Roebuck. And he was definitely no hot Italian. His red hair, freckles and glow-in-the dark white skin reminded her of an overgrown Opie Taylor. Cute, in a forty-year-old boy-next-door sort of way.

"I assume these belong to you?" he said.

Her underpants dangled from the tip of his index finger. But they weren't what caught her attention.

"Is that my purse?"

He lifted his right elbow. "I guess it is, Grace."

"How do you know my name?"

He patted her purse. "Your driver's license. The picture doesn't do you justice."

She steeled her nerves. Then she strode over and snatched the panties from the redhead's finger. "Are you a friend of Nick's?"

He snatched the panties back. "You might say that. Where is he?"

"I don't know."

"I don't believe you."

She shrugged. "It's true."

"Then what's your handbag doing in his room? Not to mention your underwear?"

"I hardly know Nick. I met him last night, at the bar. I didn't spend the night here, either. I just came to see if he'd found my ri— My purse. I thought I left it at the club, but it wasn't there when I went back for it today."

"You aren't Balboa's girlfriend?"

She shook her head.

"You didn't spend the night here?"

"No, I didn't."

"Well then. I guess this isn't yours, either."

"My ring!"

It sparkled on his pinkie, catching the small fragment of light that filtered in through a crack in the curtains.

Opie stood up. He was a full head taller than her, slim and lean and much more intimidating than when he was sitting. He moved closer. "I'll tell you what, Grace. You can have it all back, if you give me what I want."

"Oh-h." She backed toward the door. Her heart clattered in her rib cage. All remnants of her previous hangover were long gone. Damn. Why hadn't she brought her Mace?

He laughed. "Relax. I'm not going to hurt you." He stepped closer. "All I want is the key. Give me the key, and I'll give you your stuff."

"The key?" Relief washed over her. She dug into her pockets and found the room key card, holding it out to him. "No problem. Here."

He stared at it like she'd offered him a severed ear. "What's that?"

"The key card. For the room."

He exhaled through his teeth. "You know damn well that's not the key I want."

"What key do you want?" Her voice climbed higher. She could feel her heels hanging over the edge to hysteria. One more step, and she'd be gone.

"I want the memory key," he said, speaking in tones he might use with a three-year-old. "The one Nick put in your pocket last night."

She shook her head. "This is the only key he put in my pocket."

He pushed his trench coat aside to reveal a pistol strapped to his side.

"Oh, Jesus." She crossed one leg over the other. "I really have to pee."

Opie ignored her. "I saw him put it in your pocket at the bar."

He'd been at the bar. Had she talked to him? She picked through her fuzzy memory but came up with nothing.

"Did we meet last night?" she asked.

He scratched his head. "No. Just give me the friggin' memory key. Or did you and Nick sell it already?"

She laughed. She couldn't help it. It was all so absurd. So surreal. "Is this some kind of joke?" She looked around. "Are Roseanna and Cecilia in on this?"

"No, it isn't a *joke*." He backed her up against the wall.

"Oh, God. I'm sorry. I don't even know what a memory key is."

He studied her, as if debating whether or not to believe her. "Small. Rectangular. About the size of a disposable lighter."

"A lighter?" She rubbed her temples. "Wait. I found a lighter in my pocket last night in the cab. A little black one. But I couldn't figure out how to work it."

Opie looked at her through narrowed eyes.

She said, "Do you think that might have been it?"

"It's a possibility." His tone was steeped in sarcasm.

She'd heard that tone a thousand times before, from Tom. Suddenly she wasn't scared anymore. She was pissed.

"Even if I *do* have this key thing, why would I give it to you?"

"Gee, I don't know. Why would you?" He put a hand on the butt of the gun.

Okay. Back to being scared.

Opie ran his hands over her sides and down her

legs, so quickly she didn't have time to react. "You have any weapons?"

"Of course not."

He searched the pockets of her sweat jacket, coming up only with a single car key attached to a square black remote. "It's my spare. My other keys are in the handbag."

"So, where's the funny little lighter?"

"I don't have it with me."

"Where is it?"

She chewed her lip. "I'm not sure. I... I don't remember much from last night."

He stroked the pistol. "Try."

"Oh, God. I really have to pee." She bobbed from one foot to the other. "Okay. Okay. It was in the pocket of my red jacket."

"Where is that? At home?"

She felt the blood rush to her head again. Her stomach rolled over, and she sank down to a crouch. "No. It's at the Goodwill."

"The Goodwill?"

She nodded. "I put it in the bag I dropped off there this morning."

"Come on." He pulled her up by the collar of her sweat jacket. "You're driving."

"But I have to pee!"

He blew out a breath and dragged her into the bathroom. "Go ahead."

"You're kidding, right? I can't go with you *standing* there."

"Then I guess you're not going."

She gave him what she hoped was a pathetic stare.

"Damn. Alright." He collected all sharp objects and threw them into the shaving kit, which he tucked under his arm.

"I'm going to stand out in the hall with my foot in the door so you can't close it. If you try anything funny, I'll shoot right through the door. Understand?"

"Perfectly."

She tried, but she couldn't go. Not with the toe of his big, brown wingtip poking through the crack in the door.

She turned the water on, both for encouragement and to camouflage any sound.

Outside, Opie began to whistle something familiar. What was it? What…?

And suddenly, it struck her.

He was whistling "Somebody's Watching You."

CHAPTER 5.5

Saturday, 1:17 p.m.
Riding Shotgun

Pete kept his coat pocket unbuttoned so he could get to his gun, half expecting Grace to do something stupid.

He couldn't get a read on her. One minute he'd swear she was playing him, and the next he wasn't so sure. Was it possible she didn't know anything about Balboa, or the memory key?

Nope. No way.

She'd been all over Balboa like Cheez Whiz on a steak sandwich. No way she didn't know him. She had the key to his hotel room.

He had to get the memory key or kick two very long years of work to the can.

He tucked her purse beneath his arm and followed a

few steps behind her, appreciating the view as she led him to a dark green BMW sedan. She unlocked the doors with a blip of the remote.

Then suddenly, the car alarm went off, startling the crap out of him.

Christ! She wasn't as dumb as she pretended to be.

He closed the short distance between them and grabbed her arm. "Turn it off. *Now*."

"It was a mistake! I'm sorry. It won't happen again."

She punched a button on the remote and the alarm turned off with a blip. Thank God car alarms had become like political promises. Everybody heard 'em, but nobody paid any attention to them anymore.

He walked her to the passenger side door and opened it. "Get in."

She sat in the seat. He squeezed in next to her. "Climb over to the driver's side."

"You're kidding."

"Nope."

He admired her flexibility as she swung a leg over the center console. She settled into the driver's seat and gave him an expectant look.

"Now put the key in the ignition. And if you try anything funny..." He showed her the gun.

"Gee, and I was just about to recite a limerick. Have

you ever heard the one that starts 'There once was a girl from Nantucket'?"

He smiled. He couldn't help it. "Listen, all I want is the memory key. You give it to me, we're done. Understand?"

She gave him a look that said she might not believe him.

CHAPTER 6

Saturday, 1:22 p.m.
Hefty Odds

Okay. This was not a big deal.

She was driving a stranger to the Goodwill. They'd get the thingie he wanted, and then she'd get her ring and her handbag.

Her handbag, which contained the papers she'd forged for Tom.

Oh, dear God.

Her mouth went dry. This. This is what she got for being irresponsible.

She eased the car out of the parking lot, heading up Broad Street toward the Schuylkill Expressway.

Opie fiddled with the buttons on the radio. "What is this crap? Don't you have any stations grown-ups listen to?"

She punched the radio off. "If you don't mind, I'm trying to concentrate."

The traffic was crazy for a Saturday—the Flyers were playing the Rangers—taking her mind, for the moment, off the guy sitting next to her. By the time she pulled into the parking lot of the Goodwill, her hands had almost stopped shaking.

For some reason, despite the fact that he had a gun strapped just inches from her right breast, she actually believed Mr. Sears and Roebuck would do her no harm.

Unless, of course, she couldn't produce that thing he wanted. Then all bets were off.

She wasn't even sure she'd ever had it. Maybe the thing in her pocket last night really *had* been just a lighter. Then what? What were the odds he'd just let her go if she handed him a lighter?

She went woozy and put her head down on the steering wheel.

It had been so stupid to get in the car with this guy. A guy who could be a serial rapist, or a serial killer or some other kind of serial something.

And for what? For a diamond ring that could pay for a year of college? For a bunch of papers that would allow her and her children to keep their home?

Okay. Maybe she could get all that stuff back and get away. It wasn't too late.

Think. *Think*.

She could ram the car into the side of the Dumpster. Maybe the airbag would stun him for a few moments, and she could grab her purse from beside his feet and make a run for it.

"Give me the keys," he said as if he'd just read her mind.

Okay. On to Plan B.

They exited the car on the passenger side, Opie keeping a light hold on her arm as they walked across the empty parking lot.

Putting a Goodwill in South Whitpain was like putting a Talbots in South Philly. Nobody from the neighborhood would be caught dead shopping there.

She should have taken Opie down with a kick to the groin. A karate chop to the neck. An elbow to the ribs. Any one of the moves she'd mastered after watching the lady detectives in all those late-seventies detective shows.

But she didn't.

It was amazing how her inner Good Girl refused to step aside for her inner Charlie's Angel. She wanted to kick ass. She really did.

She just couldn't do anything risky. She would *not* let her children grow up with Tom and Marlene. They were bound to see something scary in that house. Something that would put them off condiments for life.

Right. On to Plan C.

She allowed Opie to escort her, largely due to the protrusion under his trench coat, straight into the building. An old cowbell tied to the door handle jingled when they entered.

She expected to see Martha behind the counter, but instead it was a guy she didn't know, working over a pile of shirts with a pricing gun.

Grace imagined grabbing the pricing gun.

Freeze, sucker. Or I'll mark you down so fast you won't know what hit you.

The clerk looked up from the shirts. "Can I help you?"

"Hi. I, uh, put a jacket into one of the bags by mistake this morning, and I need it back. Can we look for it?"

Grace attempted a psychic connection.

Call 9-1-1. Call 9-1-1!

The clerk didn't seem to get it. He opened the cash register and took a key out of one of the slots. "Donations are in the back room. Follow me."

He led them to the storeroom and opened the door. "There you go."

The floor was a sea of green trash bags that all looked as if they'd been separated at birth.

"We've had quite a few donations this weekend and nobody here to unpack them," the clerk said apologetically.

"Great. Thanks. We can take it from here," Opie said.

Grace caught the clerk's eye, trying to communicate

using her eyelids for Morse code. The clerk winked at her and left.

Only a man could mistake desperation for flirting.

"Recognize any of these bags?" Opie said.

"Yeah. The green one."

He smiled. "What time did you bring the stuff in?"

"I don't know. I usually come at ten, but I was running late this morning."

"Too many margaritas last night?"

Was that a snicker? Did she actually hear him *snicker*?

"You sound like that dog on the cartoons. You know, the one who used to have orgasms over his dog treats?"

His face clouded over. "Just find the jacket."

Grace glanced through the narrow window on the storeroom door and saw the clerk talking into the phone.

Look over here. LOOK OVER HERE.

"Get moving," Opie demanded. "Find that jacket."

She bent over and opened a bag. "What's your name, anyway?"

"What's it to you?"

She stood up. "Well, since you've been staring at my ass all afternoon, I figure the least you can do is tell me your name."

He grinned. "It's Pete, alright? Now get down to business."

His eyes crinkled at the edges when he smiled, and

Grace realized that if she wasn't afraid he'd cause her bodily harm she might actually find him attractive.

She poked through several bags, hoping she looked productive, still optimistic she'd been able to convey her sense of urgency to the clerk. She was convinced if she just stalled long enough, help would arrive.

Pete rustled through a bag. "Armani. Burberry. Moschino. I've gotta start shopping at this Goodwill." He closed the bag and opened another.

Grace stuck her hand in a bag. "Uh-h!"

"What? Did you find it?"

"No. But I could have sworn I felt something move in there."

Pete straightened, holding something red in his fist. "Is this it?"

Crap, crap, crap! How did he find it so fast? Thirty-eight bags and he nailed it, second one out. She should let him pick her lottery numbers.

She pretended to examine the jacket he held up. "No, I don't think that's mine?"

Pete shook it out and held it open. "Sure it is. I remember this gold snake on the sleeve. And this glittery stuff."

"It's a dragon. And those are called sequins." She snatched it away.

Sirens pealed in the distance. Her stomach did a little

flip. It sounded as if they were heading up Monroe, about a mile or so away.

Unfortunately, Pete heard them, too.

He narrowed his eyes. She gave him her most innocent look.

"Shit." He grabbed the jacket from her and rooted through the pockets, pulling out a small, black rectangle from one of them.

"Is that it?" she said.

"Yep." He stuck the memory key in his pocket. "Let's go."

The sirens grew louder. Pete pushed her toward the emergency exit door at the back of the storeroom.

She pushed back against him. If he managed to get her out the door, who knew what would happen in that parking lot? Screw the ring and the papers. At this point, she just wanted to get out of this without an extra hole in her body.

"You said you'd let me go when you had the key."

He grabbed her arm and dragged her to the door. "I can't exactly sit around waiting for a bus back to the city now, can I? If you'd have played nice, you'd be on your way home."

"Then just take the car and leave me here. You have what you want."

"Sorry. I need you."

"For what?"

He pushed open the lever on the emergency door. A bell, like one of those old-fashioned ball-and-hammer school bells, clanged above the door.

"You really screwed up, Grace." He shoved her through the door.

CHAPTER 6.5

Saturday, 1:35 p.m.
Sticks and Stones

Somehow she'd tipped off the clerk. It was the only explanation. She was smart, he had to give her that. And she had a great ass.

But this was inconvenient. He did *not* have time to deal with cops right now. The meeting between Nick and the Russian was supposed to go down in ten and a half hours, and there was a lot of work to do between now and then.

For one thing, he had to find Nick.

Grace suddenly sat down in the middle of the parking lot. "I'm not going with you. You can shoot me right here, but I'm not getting in that car."

"Yes, you are." He picked her up and threw her over his shoulder, firefighter style. He grabbed the remote from her hand, bleeped the car door open, then shoved her into the driver's side.

"Why do I have to drive? Just take the car. I have kids."

Outside, the sirens got louder.

He put a hand on the butt of his gun. "Look, Grace. I don't want to hurt you. Just drive the damned car."

Her eyes widened. "You can't drive a stick shift."

He could feel his face heating up, and he knew from experience that soon he'd look like a tomato with eyes. "Just drive. Get me back to the hotel."

The sirens grew louder.

"Will you give me my stuff back and let me go?"

"We'll see."

"I'm not involved in this! I don't even know Nick. I just met him last night."

"If that's true, then you have nothing to worry about. Now drive."

She gave him a defiant look.

Flashing lights reflected off the side of the Goodwill building. A maroon-and-gold police car sped into view.

And then passed.

Pete smiled. "Guess they weren't looking for us, after all."

Grace started the car. "The Baccus?"

"Please."

CHAPTER 7

Saturday, 2:02 p.m.
Pigs

What the hell is this?" Pete rolled down the car window and stuck his head out. The slightly off-key strains of "Tusk" drifted in.

"Looks like a parade."

"A parade?"

"The Columbus Day Parade. It goes right up South Broad."

"Jesus H. Christ. You've got to be kidding me."

A giant Porky Pig floated through Marconi Plaza in a sailor suit, curly tail flapping in the breeze.

Sawhorses stretched across Bigler Street, guarded by four uniformed security officers. Although truth be told, there didn't seem to be a danger that anyone would rush a giant, helium-filled pig. Or the float of dancing bananas that followed it.

"What now?" Pete muttered under his breath.

Grace rolled down the window. Pete looked at her.

"What? I'm hot."

She dangled her arm out the window, and below Pete's view waved frantically at one of the guards. He gave her a goofy smile and waved back.

While Pete looked out his window, Grace mouthed the word *help* to the guard.

He mouthed back, "Hello."

"Man!" She slapped the steering wheel.

Pete looked at her.

"I hate being stuck in traffic."

"Turn around," he said.

"You're kidding, right? There are cops right in front of us."

"They're rent-a-cops. They don't have vehicles. And even if they did, I doubt they'd care that we're breaking the U-turn law."

"There are cars behind us."

"So what? Make a K-turn."

"A *K-turn?* What the hell is a K-turn?"

He shook his head. "Don't you have a Pennsylvania driver's license? You had to do a K-turn for the test."

"Oh, yeah. I remember now. It was only twenty-two years ago. The K-turn. How could I forget?"

He shook his head. "You do have a mouth on you, don't you. You are definitely not Balboa's type."

She gave him a stony look.

"Just turn it around. Pull all the way forward. Turn the wheel to the right. Put it in Reverse. Turn the wheel again. See? You're making an invisible K with the car's wheels."

"Thank you, Mr. Reynolds."

"Who's Mr. Reynolds?"

"He was my driver's ed instructor in high school. He used to try to peek into my blouse when I was backing up."

Pete grinned his Opie Taylor grin. "An opportunist."

"A pervert."

She made one last attempt to signal the rent-a-cop leaning against the sawhorse, but he just waved again.

She stomped on the gas.

Men were pigs.

Saturday, 2:23 p.m.
X's and O's

Back at the Baccus, they parked next to a blue Ford Taurus. Pete took her keys from the ignition. "Wait here. And no funny business."

Like she was going to break out into a stand-up routine at any moment.

Hey, did you hear the one about the woman who left her twenty-thousand-dollar diamond ring in the mouth of a "mimbo"?

She rubbed her temples. She was actually getting hungry. Unlike normal people, she could eat in any situation.

The bomb—the Big One—could be on its way. While everyone else would be using their last moments to say goodbye to friends and loved ones, she'd be stuffing her face with Tastykakes. She'd be taking full advantage of the fact that no matter what she ate, very soon she'd have the same BMI as a handful of cigarette ashes.

Pete opened the trunk of the Taurus next to her car.

A Taurus? A *Taurus?*

None of the bad guys on crime shows had ever driven a Taurus.

And she was sure none of them would have ever let her pee. How could you fear a guy who drove a Taurus and let you pee?

She watched him for a little while before she realized he'd left her purse sitting on the floor, and she grabbed it. A quick search revealed two disheartening developments. One, her cell phone was dead. Two, the papers were missing.

She wondered if Nick might have them. But why in

the hell would he take those and leave her diamond ring? It didn't make sense.

She got out of the car and peered over Pete's shoulder.

The trunk was immaculate. There were four vinyl containers lined up along the back of the space, all tight and spiffy, held down by bungee cords. Grace wondered what was in them.

Pete opened the second one from the left and retrieved a laptop computer from atop a neat pile of technical-looking equipment and cables.

"This is your car?"

He straightened, smacking his head on the trunk. "Hey, get back in the car."

"Relax. I'm not going anywhere. I want my ring back."

"And you shall have it, just as soon as I'm sure this little baby is what I'm looking for." He held up the memory key.

"Why wouldn't it be?"

"I don't know. Maybe you tampered with it."

"That's right. I tampered with it. And then I put it in the pocket of a jacket I was going to give away, knowing full well that you would be in Nick's room today and that you would take me hostage at gunpoint, make me drive you to the Goodwill and force me to look through twenty bags of other people's castoffs before we eventually found it."

"Wiseass."

Pete powered up the laptop and plugged the memory key into a port in the side. He tapped a few keys. "What the hell?"

"What?" She leaned closer, peering over his shoulder at the computer screen.

It was filled with little X's and O's.

"What does that mean?" she asked.

"It means I'm screwed."

CHAPTER 7.5

Saturday, 2:29 p.m.
Shooting Blanks

Friggin' Balboa.

Pete knew in his gut that Grace wasn't lying. He knew it wasn't her who'd tampered with the key. It was Nick.

Either he'd never checked the memory key when he got it from Morton, or he'd replaced what was on it with crap. But if Balboa knew the key was essentially empty, why would he give it to Grace?

Maybe Balboa had spotted him at the club last night and had put a fake in Grace's pocket to throw him off.

No. Balboa was the kind of guy who bought condoms from a men's room vending machine. He never planned ahead.

It was more likely Morton had given Balboa the bad

key to begin with, and Balboa had just never bothered to check it.

Shit. Shit, shit, shit. Two years down the crapper. Two years, and he had nothing.

He looked at Grace.

Well, not exactly nothing. He had Balboa's girlfriend. That had to be worth something.

"Get in the car," he said, deciding to take her BMW since Balboa would recognize the blue Taurus.

"Where are we going?"

"To find your moronic boyfriend."

CHAPTER 8

Saturday, 2:47 p.m.
Sugar Sugar

Grace edged the BMW around a double-parked delivery truck.

She'd given Pete only a halfhearted argument when he'd told her to get back in the car. She was hungry and hungover and really, if she refused to go and Pete called her bluff, she didn't have much of a bargaining chip unless she was willing to get shot.

She was not. Not on an empty stomach.

She wanted a burger and french fries. She wanted another milk shake.

"Can we drive through somewhere? I'm hungry."

Pete looked at her as if she'd grown another head. "You're kidding me, right?"

She pulled over to the side of the street. "No, I'm not. I haven't eaten a thing today. I need food. I have a medical condition called hypoglycemia. Low blood sugar."

"Low blood sugar, huh? You know, that's just an excuse women use so they can be bitchy when they're hungry."

"Bitchy?" An image flashed in her mind like a movie trailer. Her, morphing into a vicious werewolf and chewing Pete's head off. "Look. I'm driving you—where?"

"Cottman Avenue."

"I'm driving you all the way across town to Cottman Avenue, largely without complaint. The least you can do is let me take a detour through a Burger King or something."

"We'll eat when we get there."

"And where is *there*?"

"The Cat's Meow."

Saturday, 3:12 p.m.
Dinner Theater

The Cat's Meow, a chartreuse, clapboard building surrounded by warehouses, pay-by-the-hour motels and fast-food joints, announced its presence with a giant pink neon cat in pasties on the roof.

"What is this?"

"One of your boyfriend's favorite hangouts. As if you didn't know."

She took a deep breath, practicing a mini-meditation, clearing all homicidal thoughts from her head. "I told you. I'm not familiar with Nick's hangouts. I'm not familiar with anything about Nick."

"You looked pretty familiar last night." Pete unbuckled his seat belt. "Let's go."

"I'm not leaving my car in this parking lot. It'll never be here when we get back."

"It'll be here."

She pressed the lock button twice, just to be sure, which she figured was about as effective as putting a sign on the window that said Please Don't Steal My Car.

Pete grabbed her purse and hooked it over her shoulder. "Here. You've been a good girl. But I'm keeping the ring for a while."

"Speaking of my things, do you have anything else that belongs to me?"

"Your panties?"

"Something else."

"Like what?"

She glanced over at him. She couldn't tell if he was genuinely curious, or fishing for information.

"Never mind," she said.

The first set of double doors led into a small foyer

with a pink linoleum floor and silver, cheetah-print wall-paper. A slick-bald bouncer in jeans, a T-shirt and a suit jacket greeted them in front of a second set of doors. Behind him on the wall were handmade posters announcing the appearances of dancers with names like Luscious Lulu and Sierra Starr.

Pete handed the bouncer two twenties—the cover charge, apparently, for the privilege of seeing what was behind Door Number Two, which Pete held open for her.

"Good God."

Can I trade for Door Number Three, Bob?

Because Door Number Two was the booby prize. Literally.

Behind the bar to their right, up on a long, narrow stage, three women of colossal proportions strolled past bar stools filled with patrons—all men—sucking beer and smiling as if they had dreams of being smothered by giant marshmallows.

"Where did they *get* those breasts?"

"Silicone Valley."

A man with slick black hair and a dark spot beneath his nose that may or may not have been a mustache approached.

"Hey, man."

Pete nodded. "Hey, Ferret. You seen Nick Balboa today?"

Ferret shook his head. "Nah. But he might be in later. It ain't like him to miss something like this."

"Go see what you can find out for me, okay?"

Ferret nodded and took off.

Pete took Grace's hand and led her to a booth in the far corner of the club.

Grace couldn't stop staring at the women on stage. It was like a train wreck. No, it was worse than a train wreck.

It was a train wreck with giant breasts.

"It's Mammoth Mammary Day at the Cat's Meow," Pete explained.

"I see that. How do they stand up with all that weight?"

"That's why they put the poles there. To give them something to hang on to. Here." He shoved a menu across the booth.

"I have to pee."

"Again?"

"Hey, you give birth to three kids and tell me how long you can go in between."

"You have three kids?"

"Yes, I do. And I really have to go again."

"In a minute." He handed her a menu. "Figure out what you want to eat before your blood sugar goes too low."

Grace scowled at him and opened the menu, trying not to think about why her fingers were sticking to the plastic cover.

"I'll have a hamburger, french fries and a milkshake."

"They don't have milk shakes here," Pete said.

"Okay, then. A Coke."

"It's a two-drink minimum per table. Why don't you order a beer?"

"Why don't *you* order a beer?"

"I don't drink."

"Neither do I."

He raised his eyebrows.

"Anymore."

A waitress in a hot-pink negligee appeared at the table.

"Hey honey, how are ya?" She winked at Pete.

"I'm good, Amber. How are you?"

"Hanging in there."

"Are you dancing tonight?" Pete said.

"Yeah. Later. After the cows go home." She jerked a thumb at the women onstage.

"You waitress *and* dance?" Grace asked.

Amber rolled her eyes. "Dincha ever hear of dinner theater?"

"You gonna order?" Pete said to Grace.

Grace gave Amber a fake smile. "I'd like a hamburger, medium, french fries and a Coke."

Amber popped her gum. "…and…a…Coke…" She scribbled on a pad. "Wow, you're brave."

"I'm hungry."

Amber smiled at Pete. "Anything for you, honey?"

"Just coffee. Thanks." Pete's gaze moved over the room.

"Is Nick here?" Grace asked.

"Do you see him?" Pete leaned back against the red vinyl seat.

"I'm afraid to look."

Amber returned with their drinks. Pete stirred a few packets of sugar into his coffee, which looked thick enough to stand a spoon in. "So, how did you get involved with Nick?"

"I'm not involved with Nick."

"You and me, we're not involved, either. Does that mean you're gonna give me your underpants and let me touch your ass?"

"You wish."

Pete took a sip of his coffee. "I want to believe you, Grace. I do. But look at it from my perspective."

She played with the straw in her Coke. "It was a game."

"A game?"

"Yes. Truth or dare. I was at the club last night with some friends from high school, and we decided to play a game of truth or dare. Relive our youth."

"So you gave Nick an expensive diamond ring on a dare?"

"Not the ring, the underwear. I gave him the ring because of the Flaming Togas."

"You're not making any sense."

She sighed. "Shots. I was drunk. I didn't know what I was doing."

"You didn't know you were kissing a stranger? Do you make a habit of kissing men you don't know?"

"No, as a matter of fact, I don't. I was just…" How could she explain what she was feeling to him? How a woman felt when she was fading. Becoming invisible.

No one looked anymore. No one whistled. And it wasn't as if she enjoyed that kind of thing, but she hadn't realized until it was gone how reassuring it had been. "Never mind. You wouldn't understand."

He gave her the strangest look, as if he actually might, and that was worse than if he didn't. She looked away in time to see the skinny guy with the smudge under his nose coming over to the booth.

"Looks like we're getting company," she said.

"Hey, Pete."

Pete made room, and the skinny guy slid onto the seat next to him.

"Grace, this is Ferret. Ferret, Grace."

"Nice to meet you, Mr. Ferret."

Ferret snorted. "Mister Ferret. That's a good one." He pushed a slip of paper over to Pete. "You might be able to find Nick at this address."

Pete nodded, and stuck the paper into his pocket. "This is Nick's girlfriend."

The man's eyes slid over her like fried eggs on Teflon. "She don't look like Nick's type." He waved Amber over. "Gimme a cheese steak and fries. And I'll take a couple beers. You know, to meet the two-drink minimum."

"You got money?" Amber said. "'Cause you ain't working it off at the door like you did last time. You let all your friends in for free."

Ferret jerked his head at Pete. "He's paying for it."

Pete nodded and took another swig of coffee.

"How good could the coffee be at a place like this?" Grace asked, as she covered her french fries with watery ketchup.

"Better than that hamburger," he said.

She bit into it.

"Ack." It tasted like roadkill. Or rather, what roadkill would taste like if it were scraped off the street, fried on a grill that hadn't been cleaned in a decade and served on a bun dating back to the Reagan administration.

"This place isn't exactly known for its food," Pete said.

"More for its theater," she said.

Pete smiled. "Right."

She ate the burger anyway, on the theory that it was better than nothing. She suspected she'd pay a hefty price for that theory later.

Ferret kept staring at her boobs, as if he didn't have enough of them to look at on the stage.

"If you gentlemen will excuse me, I have to hit the ladies' room."

"It's back there." Pete jerked a thumb toward the back of the room. "I'll be watching for you." He gave her a look fraught with meaning.

She rolled her eyes.

Saturday, 3:47 p.m.
Flushed

The ladies' room smelled like tangerine Air Wick and abandoned ambitions.

Grace tried not to touch anything. She hovered above the toilet seat, wondering how she got there.

Not only the Cat's Meow but this place where she would rather give a stranger her underwear than tell her once-best-friends that she had made a mistake a long, long time ago.

But it wasn't that long ago, was it? She'd done it again. And this time she couldn't hide behind the excuse that she was a dumb kid.

This time, she had a better excuse. She'd forged those papers for her kids. For their house. They deserved a little stability after everything that had happened this past year.

But she knew she was just sugarcoating things. What she'd done was wrong, her motives be damned.

Suddenly, she felt overwhelmed. Claustrophobic. The walls of the bathroom stall closed in on her. She grabbed one of the sanitary disposal bags stacked on the toilet tank and breathed into it.

When the dizziness passed, she staggered out of the stall. This was crazy. She shouldn't be here. She just wanted to go home and see her kids. She'd never wish for more excitement again.

On the far wall, just below a small window, a condom machine announced its offerings in bold pink letters:

RIBBED
ULTRATHIN
STUDDED
NIGHT-GLOW

Night-glow? *Night-glow?* Who would want to see something that looked like a nuclear waste accident coming at them in the dark?

A draft of cold air tickled her neck. She looked up. The window above the condom machine stood open a crack, allowing a narrow shaft of sunlight into the bathroom. Sunlight that would never get through the dirt-caked frosted glass any other way.

Grace thought she might be able to pull herself up there, and if she could...

She dragged the plastic trash can over to the wall and turned it over, dumping paper towels, lipstick-stained toilet paper and something that looked suspiciously like a body part onto the floor and climbed up on it.

The trash can wobbled. Grace caught herself on the condom machine just as the can slid out from beneath her feet.

She got a foothold on the levers of the machine and heaved herself up to the window, pushing it open with her forehead. Outside, cars raced up and down Cottman Avenue, filled with families on their way home from the mall. Families on their way home from soccer games. Families bickering about what they were going to have for dinner.

God, she wanted that.

She dove for the opening, stopping short when her hips got stuck in the window frame.

Great. She never should have eaten all those fries.

Outside, her head stuck into a sparse, dusty hedge. Inside, her legs dangled on the wall. She kicked, trying to find the condom machine, but no luck.

"You ever seen that Winnie-the-Pooh cartoon, the one where he gets stuck in the rabbit hole? I always loved that one." The voice had a sort of chain-saw-on-metal quality, not quite as melodic as Selma Diamond's from *Night Court*.

"Do you think you could help me?" Grace said.

"I guess."

Hands gripped her ankles.

"Not that way! I'll fall on you. Can you just guide my legs to the condom machine?"

The hands did as they were told.

Grace shinnied down the condom machine, past the picture of a woman who was supposed to be in the throes of an orgasm but who looked more like she was waiting for dental surgery.

She turned and came face-to-face with the oldest stripper she'd ever seen.

She must have been one of the Mammoth Mammary stars, although her mammaries had clearly migrated south, as had most of her contemporaries. Her tasseled pasties dangled just above her belly button.

Hair a bloodcurdling shade of orange stood a foot higher than her scalp, and Grace was pretty sure only a few of her teeth were real.

In that moment Grace realized that her life, which had once, long ago, resembled an episode of *Fantasy Island*, had now deteriorated into an episode of *Moonlighting*.

"Thanks for the help," Grace said.

"Sure, honey. You having a bad date?"

"Something like that." Grace wondered, could a date that was taking place at the Cat's Meow be anything *but* bad?

The dancer withdrew a tube of lipstick from her sequined hot pants and applied it while looking into the cracked mirror above the sink. "Gotta get me some of that collagen in my lips."

Right. Like that's your biggest cosmetic surgery issue.

"Hey, listen," Grace said. "Is there a back way out of here?"

"Sure. Follow me."

The old stripper scuffed along in orthopedic feath-er-trimmed mules, down a hall decorated with peeling psychedelic wallpaper. Club music, coming from beyond the wall on their right, thumped and whined like a jet engine.

Grace checked her watch. Four oh-five. Kevin would be on the soccer field, looking for a way to avoid the ball. She wondered if Tom was there, too, looking for a way to avoid her parents and probably looking for her and the forged papers.

The bastard. This was all his fault.

If he had never come selling pharmaceuticals at the doctor's office where she'd worked as a summer temp, she never would have met him. And if he hadn't asked her out the day after she'd seen *Pretty Woman*—he looked a lot like Richard Gere—she never would have gone out with him.

If she hadn't gone out with him, she never would have slept with him, and then she certainly never would have married him, couldn't have found him in flagrante delicto with his assistant, wouldn't have divorced him, never would have forged those papers and, thus, never would have felt compelled to let loose with her friends at a cheesy nightclub in a desperate attempt to get the whole damned mess off her mind.

Bastard.

She followed the stripper past a little room off the corridor lined with mirrors and a folding table with a duct-taped leg. Women revealing varying amounts of skin milled about, smoking cigarettes and applying eye makeup.

"That's where we girls get dressed," the stripper informed her.

Wouldn't that be *undressed?* Grace wondered.

They passed an area that was cold and smelled oddly like curry. And at long last they reached an old, gray door. Above it in faded red paint were the words *Fire Exit.*

Nothing like being safety conscious.

"This is it. You sure you want to go out there, honey? Alone?"

"Absolutely."

Grace cracked the door. The fresh air was intoxicating, despite its abundance of fine particulates and nearly double the recommended parts per million of ozone. Philadelphians liked air they could sink their teeth into.

Grace gave the old dancer a nod of thanks and stepped out into the sunshine.

The door slammed shut behind her.

She turned, only to find Pete leaning up against the brick wall, smoking a cigarette. "Well, well. I started to get worried when you didn't come back for dessert. You seem like the kind of woman who eats dessert."

"Shit."

Pete grabbed her arm. "Come on. We have to find your boyfriend, then you're off the hook. Maybe."

"He's not my boyfriend."

"Right." They made their way around the building and back to the parking lot. Pete pushed the button to open the car doors, and the car answered back with a flash of the parking lights.

Tires squealed. Grace and Pete froze, caught in the path of a blue-and-white police cruiser that came to a stop inches in front of them, so close Grace could feel the heat from the car's hood on her thighs.

"Holy—"

Pete clutched her arm.

Cops leaped out of both sides of the car, and two seconds later, another cruiser pulled up behind them.

"Get your hands up." One of the cops, gun drawn, approached them from behind.

"Are you Grace Marie Becker?"

"Yes."

"And who are you?" The cop grabbed Pete's arm and pushed him up on the hood of the car.

"Pete Slade. Can I ask why you're detaining us?"

"Certainly. We got a call from the South Whitpain police, asking for assistance in looking for this woman's car. A clerk at the Goodwill reported suspicious behavior. Said you might be holding this woman against her will."

"I was. I am. But I have good cause."

The cop snorted. "I'll bet you do."

Pete sighed. "I guess we'd better straighten this out at the station."

CHAPTER 8.5

Saturday, 4:49 p.m.
Coming Out

Pete ground his teeth. He could feel a migraine starting behind his left eye.

Balboa was supposed to meet Skobelov at midnight tonight to give him the memory key. But Pete didn't have Balboa *or* the memory key, and pretty soon he wasn't going to have a job.

The cuffs bit into his wrists as he turned around in the backseat of the cruiser, trying to get a look at the car behind them. The car Grace was riding in.

He wondered what she was telling the cops. And he wondered how she'd tipped off the clerk at the Goodwill.

Damn. He didn't have time for this. And on a holiday

weekend, too. Everything was going to take twice as long as it should.

But, hey. Nothing had gone smoothly with this case. Nothing at all. Why should that change now?

CHAPTER 9

Saturday, 7:37 p.m.
Catching Knives

"You're a *Secret Service* agent?"

"Yep."

Grace gripped the edges of the plastic chair in the small interrogation room where she'd been waiting. "Shouldn't you be guarding the president's dog or something?"

"That's a common misconception. The United States Secret Service has a number of responsibilities."

"But why didn't you tell the police who you were? Why did you let them arrest you?"

"They didn't arrest me. They detained me, which they were going to do anyway until they checked my credentials to make sure I really am who I say. For my own purposes, it was better to be cuffed in front of the Cat's Meow than to be seen showing the cops an ID."

"So why didn't you tell *me* who you were? Where do you get off, dragging me around like you're some sort of dangerous felon, scaring the crap out of me?"

"I'm sorry, Grace. But I had no way of knowing who you were. I would have put myself and the investigation at risk."

"You could have just let me go."

"Why would I do that?"

"Because I don't have anything to do with whatever you're investigating."

"So you claim."

"I've been telling you all along, I don't know Nick Balboa. I went to the hotel to get my stuff. That's all."

Pete straddled the chair across from her at the scarred wooden table. "I'd like to believe that, Grace. But I just can't."

"You can't? Why the hell not?"

"Because, as I said before, the Secret Service is responsible for investigating many types of crimes. Financial institution fraud, computer fraud, money laundering, counterfeiting. Identity theft. Those types of things."

Grace's heart stopped. "What does this have to do with me?"

Pete opened the folder he'd brought in with him.

"Grace Marie Poleiski Becker. Born September twenty-first, nineteen—"

"Cut to the chase, please."

He turned the folder around and pushed it toward her. "You have a record for forgery and identification theft."

A pain seared through her stomach. It could have been from the burger she'd eaten at the Cat's Meow, but somehow she doubted it. "That was a long time ago."

"Not long enough, apparently."

"It was a mistake. I was young. We were making IDs so our friends could get into bars."

Pete leaned back in the chair. "Here's the thing, Grace. I used to think you weren't Nick's type, being so ol—. Being so mature and all. But, according to your record, it would seem you're exactly his type."

Grace was silent.

"What was the plan? He was going to steal the names on the key, and you were going help him make up counterfeit identification?"

"*What?*"

"IDs. False documents. From the names and social security numbers on the memory key."

"I didn't even know what a memory key was before today. I swear."

"But you know what false identification is, don't you? You know how to make it. You know how to forge names."

Grace's throat began to close up. Tears stung the back of her eyelids. "What do you want me to say?"

"I want you to say you'll help me find Nick. And then we'll figure out what to do with you."

"I think I should call my lawyer."

Pete shrugged. "Sure. But you're not officially under arrest yet. If you want to call your lawyer, I'll put you under arrest for suspicion of identification fraud and computer fraud." He looked at the clock. "Being that it's a holiday weekend, you should be out by, say, Tuesday afternoon."

Grace traced her fingertip over a little drawing of Kilroy someone had inked on the table a hundred years ago.

She wanted this all to be a bad dream.

She wanted to wake up next to Tom, with his damp feet and nasal strips, and look out over a backyard littered with soccer balls and Hula-Hoops. In fact, a fourth-grade flute concert was looking pretty good at the moment.

She burst into tears. What was she going to tell the kids?

Pete shifted uncomfortably in his chair. "Come on. Don't cry. I'm not really interested in small fry like you. I'm after the Russian. Even Nick will probably walk, provided he decides to cooperate. I can't get to Skobelov without him. I just need you to convince him to play nice from now on."

"But I told you—"

"Yeah, yeah. I know. You don't know Nick." Pete slammed her file closed in disgust.

Grace rubbed her forehead. "Can I have a minute to think about all this?"

"Sure. But a minute is all we got."

Pete left the room.

Grace swallowed and opened her file. A mug shot of a younger, cockier version of herself stared back at her.

That Grace, twenty-year-old Grace, wouldn't sit here crying. *That* Grace would tell off Pete Slade, Secret Service agent. She'd spend the weekend in jail just to spite him.

But *that* Grace hadn't been to jail yet.

Jail was not a nice place. Just ask Martha Stewart. No matter how hard the maven of style may have tried to make it nice, it just wasn't. Maxi-pad slippers and toilet-paper roll wreaths couldn't dress the place up enough to hide the cold, gray walls and unbearable loneliness.

And Grace—*today's* Grace—did not want to go back.

She'd only spent three weeks in jail, but to say they were the worst three weeks of her life was like the Black Knight in *Monty Python and the Holy Grail* saying, "It's just a flesh wound!" when his arm was cut off.

And if she opted to stay in jail, she had absolutely no chance of getting those forged papers back from Nick. She definitely did *not* want those floating around. Specifically not now that she knew who Pete was.

Nope. No way. She was not going to sit behind bars and wait for the proverbial shoe to drop.

She couldn't help Pete. She knew that. But he didn't. And if it meant keeping her butt out of jail, she could pretend, couldn't she?

She would just have to look at all of this as an adventure. Flirting with disaster. Like the rush the person hanging on a knife-thrower's spinning target might feel when she sees a nine-inch blade hurtling toward her face.

Grace wiped the tears from her cheeks with the sleeve of her sweatshirt, leaving a streak of black from her mascara.

Pete came back into the room, closing the door behind him. "What'll it be?"

"Okay. I'll give it a shot."

Saturday, 8:08 p.m.
Face-lifting

"Why don't we check the hotel again?" Grace suggested, hoping she could look for her papers. Maybe she'd missed them somewhere in Nick's room.

"Nah. Balboa won't be there," Pete said.

"So, where to then?"

"You tell me."

Grace was just about to reiterate the fact that she had no idea, when one actually came to her.

"What about the address Ferret gave you?"

Pete pulled the slip of paper from his shirt pocket. "Catharine Street."

They drove to the Italian Market area of Philadelphia, which was always busy on the weekends. During the day, vendors sold fresh fruits and vegetables from carts and tables lining the streets. Cheese shops, pasta shops, butchers and bakers propped their doors open for the never-ending stream of customers.

And in the evening, the restaurants came alive.

Grace's stomach growled loudly.

"Don't tell me you want to eat again," Pete said.

She did, but that wasn't why they were there.

"I know where we are," Pete said. "Nick's family owns this place. He told me he liked to hang out here in the kitchen when he was kid. Like five years ago."

"He's not *that* young." Grace said as she searched for a parking spot while diners milled around on the sidewalk in front of a little bistro, waiting to get a seat inside.

"He's not that old, either," Pete retorted.

She worked the BMW into a tight spot near the front of the bistro. She'd always had good parking karma.

"So, go on," Pete said. "Go get him."

"*Me?*"

"Sure. What do you think he'd do if he saw me?"

"I don't know, and I don't care. I'm not getting involved in this."

Pete snorted. "Lady, you're already involved. You're in so deep you should be wearing diving gear."

"Very funny." She rubbed her forehead. "How am I supposed to get him out here? That is, if he's even in there."

"Not my problem. Just do it quick."

Grace checked her face in the rearview mirror. The makeup she'd so haphazardly applied twelve hours ago, when she'd been hung over and much, much happier, looked ghastly. Her yoga pants were streaked with dirt from her expedition scaling Mount Trojan, and her sweatshirt sleeves were stained with mascara.

"You look great," said Pete.

She gave him a bitchy look and opened the car door. "How can you be so sure I'm not going to take off?"

"It hasn't seemed to work for you so far."

"Yeah, well, there's a first time for everything."

She slammed the car door shut and pushed her way through the tight crowd on the sidewalk, ignoring dirty looks from hungry women and dodging the men who looked like gropers.

At the hostess station inside the door, a pretty young woman with big, dark curls and deadly looking three-inch spiked heels asked for her name.

"I'm looking for Nick Balboa," Grace said. "He told me he sometimes hangs out here."

"Who are you?"

"I'm his...uh, I'm his girlfriend."

The hostess laughed. "Right."

"I am."

The young woman put a hand on one hip, showcasing long, red nails. "One night of staring at yourself in the mirror above Nick's bed doesn't make you his girlfriend. Besides, aren't you a little old for him?"

"I'm not *that* old." Grace did the instant face-lift thing. The one on the infomercial where some aging soap opera star explains how to tighten certain muscles in your face to look ten years younger in an instant.

Maybe it worked. Or maybe the hostess felt sorry for her because she said, "Hang on. I'll go see if he's here."

A few minutes later, Nick materialized through the swinging door that led to the kitchen. He smiled, and Grace's stomach lurched.

Had she really made out with this demigod? This vision of male perfection?

The thought gave her the shivers.

She did the instant face-lift thing again as he approached.

"Man, am I glad to see you," he said. "Where did you disappear to last night?"

The scent of garlic and Bolognese clung to him like cologne. She moved closer. It was even better than Aramis. "I had to get home. Emergency."

He nodded. "I think I put something in your pocket by mistake."

She went for an innocent look, hoping she could pull it off while still face-lifting. "That little black thingie?"

"Yeah. Exactly. You still got it?"

She nodded. "It's at my place. Why?"

"I need it as soon as possible."

"Do you have my purse? And my ring?"

"They're back at my room."

She tucked a finger under the collar of his shirt. "I'll tell you what. We'll go by the hotel and pick up my stuff, and then I'll take you back to my place and get that thing for you."

"Sounds like a plan." Nick smiled. The wattage could have put a disco ball to shame.

When they passed the hostess station, Nick said, "Hey, Elaina. Tell Aunt Aida I'll be back in a little while."

"Sure." Elaina gave Grace a shrug and a look that implied wonders never ceased.

Nick put his hand on her waist as they hit the sidewalk and guided her through the crowd of waiting patrons. Grace's stomach fluttered, as much from Nick's touch as from the fact that she knew what was going to happen.

Or was it?

Pete wasn't waiting in the car.

What was she supposed to do now? Throw Nick down on the sidewalk and tie him up with her shoelaces?

Come to think of it, the idea did have its merits. But this was neither the time nor the place…

"Hello, Nick." Pete's voice came from behind them.

"Damn," said Nick.

"Funny, that was my thought exactly when you didn't call me this morning. Where are the names you're supposed to have for Skobelov tonight?"

"You know, funny thing. I didn't get the memory key. Morton never met me in Boise."

"Bullshit."

"He wasn't at the motel. I—"

"Cut the crap, Nick. I saw you put the memory key into Mrs. Robinson's pocket last night at Caligula. And I got the feeling you knew I was watching you, or you wouldn't have done it."

Nick shrugged. "Then I guess you got the names."

"No. I got the memory key, but there weren't any names on it. Just a love note from Morton for Skobelov. Lots of X's and O's."

"You're kidding." Nick looked genuinely stunned. "But I checked the key at the hotel. The names were there."

"You checked it?"

131

"Of course. What do you think? I'm stupid?"

Pete exhaled. "You checked it, and then you never let it out of your sight?"

"No—" Nick stopped short. "Damn. That little weasel. I can't believe he double-crossed me."

"Just like you double-crossed me?"

Nick held out his arms. "Hey, Pete. It wasn't like that."

"Then explain it to me, Nick. Because from where I stand it looks like you were gonna take the names for yourself and maybe get a little side business going with your girlfriend, here."

Nick looked at Grace and then back at Pete. "Nah. I was just gonna sell the key to the highest bidder."

"Thank *you*," Grace said. "The truth finally comes out. I *told* you I had nothing to do with this."

Pete shrugged. "We'll see."

"What now?" Nick asked. "You gonna arrest me?"

Pete opened the back door of the BMW. "I don't know. Get in."

CHAPTER 9.5

Saturday, 8:21 p.m.
Gin Fizz

Pete felt like his head had gone through a garbage disposal. But that was the least of his worries.

He had an informant he couldn't trust, a case he didn't think was strong enough and a woman he didn't know, period.

If things didn't come together soon, they were going to blow apart. It was the law of Order and Chaos. Either this all was meant to be, or it wasn't. And the next twenty-four hours were going to decide that.

Up front, Nick slipped his arm over the back of Grace's seat and sang some song that Pete vaguely remembered. Something from his early college days. Van Halen. "Why Can't This Be Love."

Pete remembered it because he'd sung it, in a drunken stupor, to a gorgeous Phi Mu named Barbara at the one and only fraternity party he'd ever attended.

He'd thought the sun rose on her gorgeous pair of breasts and set on her luscious behind. She'd thought he was a hopeless loser, unfit even to lick the gin fizz she'd spilled on her white cowboy boots.

Her boyfriend apparently had thought so, too.

Pete had ended up hanging upside down from the frat house flagpole, his pants in a knot around his neck and his mouth duct taped shut.

It was a moment of supreme humiliation but also one of self-realization.

If he were to ever make it through college and, indeed, the "real world" alive, he would definitely have to become the strong, silent type.

It had worked, for the most part.

But, every once in a while, he was tempted to lick the gin fizz off of some woman's boots and tell her the "mook" she was with wasn't worth the cologne he was steeped in.

Nick twirled a lock of Grace's hair between his fingers, and Pete looked away. He swallowed a couple Tylenol, dry, and chased them with a Tums.

Screw it. He'd spent the last two years alone, focusing completely on this case. And now, so close to the end, he wanted to risk getting run up the flagpole for some broad with a smart mouth and a nice smile?

Forget about it.

It was time to get his head back in the game.

CHAPTER 10

Saturday, 8:36 p.m.
Getting Hot

They drove only a few blocks from the Italian Market before Pete told Grace to park.

"Where are we?" she asked.

"My place."

Grace and Nick followed Pete half a block to a redbrick row house, with one red door and one blue. He opened the blue one with a key, and stuck his head in the door. "Louis, it's me."

Pete led them into a foyer with wide wood-plank floors and silver-blue painted walls. Decoupage wall sconces cast indirect light onto the ceiling, giving the entryway a warm feel despite the cool colors.

"Who's Louis?" Nick sniggered. "Your life partner?"

Pete looked over Nick's shoulder. "Hey, Lou. You my life partner?"

A man slightly smaller than the Chrysler Building, with a stare that could freeze antifreeze, filled the hallway.

Nick postured for a few seconds, but when Louis trained hard, black eyes on him, all the wind went out of Nick's sails.

Pete clapped his hand on Nick's shoulder and said to Louis, "This is the jerk-wad who screwed up two friggin' years of work."

"Hey, watch the shirt," Nick said, without much conviction.

"So what do we do now, boss?" Louis asked.

"I don't know. I need a beer."

"I thought you said you didn't drink," said Grace.

"I'm making an exception," said Pete.

They all filed into a neat little galley kitchen with maple cabinets and stainless steel appliances that looked brand new. Set up on a small table in the corner was enough electronic equipment to make the place look like the *Star Trek* command center.

"Anything going on?" Pete said to Louis.

"Nah. The Russian left his apartment about an hour ago."

"You got the place bugged?" Nick said.

Pete and Louis ignored him.

Pete opened up the refrigerator, revealing two six-packs of beer, a bottle of ketchup, an open can of succotash and something lying on the bottom shelf that looked like it could win the starring role in the next *Alien* movie.

Grace itched to get her fingers on Pete's appliances. What she couldn't do with a double convection oven.

Okay. How sad was that? The thought of using a guy's stove was making her hot. She unzipped her sweatshirt.

Three pairs of male eyes immediately focused on her chest. She zipped her sweatshirt back up.

They all sat on wrought iron bar stools around the tiny breakfast bar.

Pete passed the beers around. "Okay, here's how I see it. Nick has to keep the meeting with Skobelov. Business as usual, just like we planned."

"But I don't have the memory key," Nick protested. "And even if I did, didn't you just tell me there was nothing on it?"

"Yeah, but you've got to convince him he's still going to get the names."

Nick shook his head. "No way. I'm not gonna lie to Viktor Skobelov. He's fucking scary, man."

"Oh, but you were going to steal thirty-thousand names and social security numbers out from under him? What if he knew that, Nick, huh? What if he knew you were gonna cross him?" Pete took a swig of his beer.

"You wouldn't..." Nick looked at Pete and then at Louis. Louis was smiling.

Nick pulled on his earlobe. "What if I say no?"

Pete shrugged. "You can do that. We'll just have to get you into witness protection as soon as possible, so you can testify against Skobelov when I finally do manage to make a case against him, probably in two years or so. You'll love Kansas, Nick."

"What if I say no?"

"Not an option. It's testifying or jail. That was our deal, Nick. And believe me, the Secret Service does not take kindly to those who mess up our cases. We'll push for the maximum sentence. Right, Lou?"

Louis iced Nick with his stare.

Nick looked at Grace. "What do you think I should do, honey?"

"Me?"

"I'm not talking to Louis."

Grace gave Nick the evil eye. "Can I see you in the other room, *honey?*"

Saturday, 8:54 p.m.
The Viagra Papers

"Are you out of your mind?" Grace said, through clenched teeth. "Why are you dragging me into this?"

139

Nick raised one shoulder. "I just wanted your opinion."

"You want my opinion? Why?"

"I don't know. You seem like you got a good head on your shoulders."

"Oh, sure." She had a feeling Nick missed the sarcasm in her reply.

"Listen," Nick said. "This wasn't the way things were supposed to go between us. Why didn't you meet me back at the room?"

"Because I came to my senses."

Nick ran his hands through his hair. "You were supposed to come back to the room with the memory key. If you had, none of this would've happened."

"Well, why'd you put it in my pocket to begin with? What made you so sure I was going to come to your room?"

Nick gave her a look she hadn't seen since the Fonz on *Happy Days*. She imagined him in a leather jacket, hair slicked back, saying "A-a-ay-y-y."

Grace put her hand on her hip. "Oh, I get it. *Of course* I would come back to your room. A middle-aged soccer mom desperate for a hot night with a young stud. Is that it?"

Nick shrugged. "I thought we had something going."

Grace took a deep, cleansing breath. And another and another. "You said you want my opinion? If I were you, I'd just cooperate with them. Do whatever they want."

"Why?"

"Why?"

"Yeah, why?"

"Because… Because it's the right thing to do."

Nick smiled. "You always do the right thing?"

"I try to."

"Uh-huh."

"What's that supposed to mean?"

Nick reached out and tucked a curl behind her ear. "Let's just say I got a look at some papers that might prove differently."

Grace's body began to buzz. "Papers?"

"Papers that release a large quantity of Viagra to a new 'vendor.'"

Viagra? Was that what this whole thing was about? Tom needed Viagra?

She hadn't read the papers before she signed them. She didn't want to know what he was up to. But this was crazy. It didn't make any sense. Tom would never risk all of this for Viagra. Would he?

An image of him with Marlene and a giant tub of mayonnaise flashed through her head.

That asshole. That stupid asshole.

"I don't know what papers you're talking about," she said to Nick.

"The ones you forged, Grace."

"Prove it."

Nick grinned. "I have a ringing endorsement from your husband."

"Tom?"

"You have another husband?" Nick slid his hand behind her neck and pulled her close, kissing her lightly. "Do you think meeting me was an accident?" he whispered.

"Oh, God…" She didn't want to hear this. "How—?"

"Hey!" Pete shouted from the kitchen. "You done in there? 'Cause we've got to have an answer. Now."

CHAPTER 10.5

Saturday, 9:08 p.m.
X Factor

C'mon, *Balboa. Gimme the right answer.*

Pete picked at the label on his beer bottle and tried to look bored.

The truth was, without Nick Balboa, he didn't have much of a case. They could get the Russian, Skobelov, on a few minor fraud charges, but they needed the big pop.

The Russian was too well-protected. Pete knew he was involved in some pretty heavy stuff: money laundering, immigration violations, Internet drug sales. But the only thing Pete cared about was the identification fraud. It was the cornerstone of his investigation. All the rest was gravy.

The Russian had put up sixty grand for names he'd bought from Morton, a computer geek who worked at a credit card processing center in Boise, Idaho.

The plan was simple. Balboa was supposed to fly out to Boise, pick up the memory key from Morton and bring it back to Philly. Then Pete would copy the information, enter it into evidence and, when Skobelov used the names for fraudulent purposes, they'd have him dead to rights.

But without Balboa, he couldn't pull it off. Balboa was his inside man. The only one he knew who could get close to Skobelov.

But even if Balboa agreed to stay in, who was to say he wouldn't cross them again? He was the loose cannon. The X factor.

Right now, the stupid jerk had his hand linked in Grace's, who looked like she might chew her arm off to get away from him. Pete himself could have happily ripped Balboa's head off.

He'd really begun to hope Grace wasn't a part of all this. He'd wanted to believe her, but her arrest record made it unlikely. He was inexplicably disappointed.

"Well, what's it gonna be, Nick?"

Balboa sucked down the last of his beer and plunked the bottle down on the counter. "I'll do it."

CHAPTER 11

Saturday, 9:35 p.m.
Big Red Nose

"I have to make a call."

Pete looked at her like she was insane.

"I have to call my kids. My mother. They'll be worried if I don't."

Pete thought for a minute. "Lou, go with her. Let her use the kitchen phone." He went back to hooking a small device to the inside of Nick's collar.

Grace followed Louis to the kitchen, where he pointed to an old-fashioned wall phone with a long, curly cord. It was exactly like the phone her parents used to have in their kitchen. Grace used to stretch it into the pantry, where she'd close the door, eat Oreos and talk to Cecilia and Dannie all night.

"Make it quick," Louis said.

Grace dialed slowly, trying to think of what she was going to say. Her heart bounced around in her chest like a Super Ball. Megan answered the phone.

"Hi, sweetie. How's it going?"

"Pretty lame. Grandma wouldn't even let me go to the mall, and I *have* to get a dress for homecoming. I mean, *when* am I supposed to do *that*?"

"We'll go on Tuesday, okay?"

As long as I'm not in jail. Or swimming with the fishes.

Grace's voice broke. "I promise we'll go. Just you and me."

"Jeez, Mom. It's only a dress. You don't have to cry about it."

Grace wiped her nose on her sleeve. "Is Grandma there?"

"Yeah, hang on."

The phone clunked. A television blared in the background, and it was several minutes before her mother came on.

"Hello, dear."

"Hi, Mom. Am I interrupting something?"

"No, no. We're just watching *Terms of Endearment*. It's almost to the part where Shirley MacLaine's yelling at the nurses, 'Give her the shot! Give my daughter the shot!' So sad."

"How are the kids?"

"They're fine. How was your night out with your friends?"

"Interesting, I guess."

"Does Cecilia still have such a fresh mouth? I remember she once told me to—"

"Mom, that was twenty years ago."

"Well, still. You never get over something like that. By the way, I tried to call your cell phone, but I got the voice mail."

"Yeah. It wasn't charged up."

"I was getting worried. Tom's been calling here for you." She lowered her voice to a whisper. "I can't believe he has the nerve."

Louis nudged Grace with his elbow.

"Listen, Mom. I have to get going—"

"Oh, look. It's the part where Debra Winger is telling the little boy she won't be coming home. You always cry at this part, and your nose gets all big and red."

"Mom, I really have to go."

Her mother sighed. "Okay, then. Callie and Kevin are in bed, but do you want to talk to Megan again?"

"Sure. Real quick." She dodged Louis's elbow and gave him a look.

Megan came on the line. "Yes, Mother?"

"Megan, I want you to help Grandma with Callie and

Kevin." The tears started again, and Grace imagined her nose swelling to twice its size.

"Mom, are you crying again? Jeez, take a pill."

"Just be good, okay?"

"Like, when am I ever not good? Can I go now?

Grace sniffed. "Go ahead. Tell Grandma I said goodbye."

Grace hung up the phone and looked at Louis. "What's in these cabinets? I really need to cook something."

Saturday, 10:44 p.m.
Rash Thoughts

"This is awesome." Nick shoveled food into his mouth while bent over the sink, a paper napkin tucked into his collar so as not to short out the body bug he was wearing.

Grace had discovered a pound of hamburger in the freezer and an onion in the hydrator tray. Along with a couple of cans of succotash and a few squirts of ketchup, she'd managed to pull together a half-decent goulash. But the urge to cook still hadn't subsided.

"Not bad, Gracie," Pete said. "You a professional chef or something?"

"No. And please don't call me that."

"What? Gracie?"

"My ex-husband calls me Gracie. I can't stand it."

"Is he the one who gave you this nice diamond ring? 'Cause I know it wasn't Nick, here." Pete wiggled the ring on his finger.

"Hey," Nick said. "It could've been me."

Louis's spoon stopped midway to his mouth. "Heh."

Nick shook his head. "Why is it so hard to believe that I gave my lady friend here a gift?"

"I am not your 'lady friend,'" Grace said.

"Okay, okay. My *woman*."

The protest was on her lips, but before she could get the words out, Nick leaned over and kissed her.

The scent of Aramis rendered her momentarily unable to function. She sat there, helpless, as Nick's bionic lips moved over hers.

When Nick finally pulled away, Pete's expression was black. "Save it for later. We gotta roll."

"How about giving me my ring back now?" Grace said.

"Later." Pete put the ring in his pants pocket. "Insurance."

Pete and Louis collected some complicated-looking electronic gadgets and loaded them into a big, black duffel bag.

"We'll stop by the hotel first, so I can get my car," Pete said. "Then Lou will take the two of you on to the meeting place."

"Where are *you* going?" Grace said.

"Boise. See if I can track down Morton."

"I hope you find him," Grace said. "I really do." Because maybe then she could go home.

The thought brought relief and just a teeny sliver of regret. She had to admit, she hadn't felt this alive in a long, long time.

Her role as Tom's wife required a sophisticated hostess, not a party girl. A woman who could hold a conversation, not one who could tell jokes.

But, sometime in the last twenty-four hours, her impulsive side had been resuscitated.

The four of them piled into Grace's car and drove to the Baccus Hotel. Pete and Nick went in and retrieved the rest of Nick's things. Pete put everything into the trunk of Grace's car and leaned in the driver's side window to talk to Louis.

He smelled of decent cologne. It was no Aramis, true. But Grace was surprised by his choice. He had the beginnings of reddish beard stubble growing on his chin, like an unkempt version of David Caruso. It was the kind of stubble that could give a girl a nasty rash…

Whoa. Where had that *come from?*

She already had one more imaginary boyfriend than she wanted. The thought of getting a rash, or anything else, from Pete Slade was strictly verboten.

"Don't screw this up," Pete said to Nick. "Louis will

be listening. If you get into trouble, remember the emergency word."

"Pineapple."

"Right. But only if you're in trouble. Convince him, Nick. Convince Skobelov the names are on the way."

"Sure."

Grace could see Nick's face in the rearview mirror. He didn't look so sure. In fact, he looked like he was about to puke.

Pete slapped the roof of the car. "Go get 'em."

Saturday, 11:51 p.m.
Eavesdropping

Back to the Cat's Meow.

The neon cat on the roof seemed to be running out of juice, its winking eye more closely resembling a palsy twitch than a seductive gesture.

"What time is it?" Nick asked.

"Five of," Louis said. "You ready?"

"Yeah." Nick got out of the car and leaned in Grace's window, just as Pete had done. "Can I have a kiss for good luck?"

Her stomach knotted. "You're kidding me, right?"

Nick flashed his thousand-watt smile. "You want me to be kidding you?"

She hit the button to roll up the window.

Nick straightened his collar and headed for the door of the club. Grace had a hard time keeping her eyes off his butt.

"Now what?" she said to Louis.

He rooted through the bag and pulled out a black box the size of a hardcover book and plugged it into the cigarette lighter with an adapter. "Now, we listen."

"What is that thing?"

"A receiver. It records everything that comes over the body wire."

Louis opened the lid of the box, revealing a row of knobs and buttons. He hit one and it crackled to life, lights jumping in little bars across the face of a tiny screen. A rhythmic sound spewed from the box.

"What's that noise?" Grace said.

"Nick's breathing. I guess that's a good thing, huh?" He snickered to himself. Just then it struck her who Louis reminded her of. The old detective Fish, from *Barney Miller*.

They heard "Hey, Nick."

"The bouncer at the door," Louis said.

Blaring music. The Pussycat Dolls.

"Hi, Nicky."

"Hey, Shannon. Looking good."

"Hey, Nick."

"Lisa, wow. Nice dress."

"He's smooth," Louis said. Grace thought she detected a tiny note of admiration in his tone.

"Nicky, where you been?"

"Hey, Maria. Where's the boss?"

"He's waiting for you at the back booth."

"Thanks."

"Here we go," Nick muttered under his breath.

For a few moments, all they could hear was the sound of dance music pumping in the background.

"Nicholas. How is the car running?"

"It's the Russian," said Louis to Grace, as if she couldn't hear the accent.

"Car's running great," they heard Nick say. "Just got some new rims. I'm gonna show her at the Classic Car Expo."

"Good. Good. She's a beauty." Belch. "You remember Tina?"

"Of course. How are you, honey?"

"Couldn't be better."

"So, Nicky," said Skobelov. "How was your trip? You got something for me?"

Nick beat a rhythm on the table with his fingers. "Morton screwed us over, Viktor."

Bass thumped in the background. "What you mean, screwed us over? You don't have?"

"Nah. I got to the hotel near the airport and Morton

153

wasn't there. Maybe he was being followed or something. I have a friend working on it."

"A friend?"

"Yes. A good friend. One who can be trusted."

"I don't trust nobody. I don't trust you."

"You can trust me, Viktor. I'll get the names."

"I should kill you. You know that?"

"I know. I know. But it wasn't my fault. I'll have what you want by tomorrow."

A long pause. "What you think, Tina?"

"Ah, give him till tomorrow. What's it gonna hurt?"

Ice cubes clinking in a glass. Music thumping.

"Tomorrow," Skobelov said. "If you got no names, I won't be happy. First, I cut your fingers off. Then your pretty nose. Then we see what else stick out, eh?"

Skobelov's laughter faded and the music grew louder. Grace could hear the sound of Nick walking away from the table. Fast.

"Nice guy," Louis said, switching off the receiver as Nick emerged from the club's front door. He hightailed it across the parking lot and climbed into the backseat of Grace's car.

Nobody said anything.

Grace wondered what the men were thinking. Because she knew what she was thinking.

Holy shit.

Sunday, 2:35 a.m.
The Chopping Block

They were about a block from Pete's place when they passed the all-night supermarket. Louis was in the driver's seat. Grace didn't think her nerves could handle it.

"Pull over here," Grace said.

"What for?" Louis asked.

"You have to eat, don't you? And I have to cook. But just about all that's left in that kitchen are a few packets of soy sauce and a banana. Even I can't do much with that."

"You heard her. Pull over, Louis," said Nick. "The lady needs to cook."

Louis double-parked in front of the grocery store.

Grace was in and out in fifteen minutes, struggling to the car with three big paper bags of groceries.

"What'd you get?" said Louis, grabbing the bags and throwing them in the backseat next to Nick.

"You'll see."

Back at Pete's, Grace shed her coat and shoes, poured herself a glass of wine before she remembered her vow never to drink again and went to work. She watched Nick out of the corner of her eye, waiting for a chance to talk to him when Louis wasn't lurking nearby.

"You want to help me chop, here?" she said to Nick.

155

"Sure." He unbuttoned the sleeves of his silk shirt and rolled them up to his elbows.

She never knew a man's wrists could be so sexy. She took a gulp of wine.

In the other corner of the kitchen, near the command center, Louis turned on a small television set and flipped through the channels before settling on a late-night western. He propped his feet up on a chair and opened a bag of potato chips.

Trying to keep her voice beneath the sound of galloping horses and the *ping-pings* of gunshots, Grace said to Nick, "Maybe we should finish our conversation from before."

"What conversation?"

"Hello? The one where you insinuated you know my ex-husband?"

"I didn't insinuate anything. I do know your ex-husband. I met him at a car show about six months ago. He's the one who got me thinking that we should hook up."

"*What?*"

"That you and I should get together."

"Jesus! Does he think I'm so desperate for a date that *he* has to set me up? What a sick f—"

"Hey, he didn't try to set us up like *that*." Nick grinned. "That was my idea."

Now she was confused. "I'm not following you."

Nick looked over at Louis. He'd fallen asleep, head tipped back, mouth open, potato chip crumbs on his shirt.

"Tom and I were talking one time about your...*skills*. I got to thinking that maybe I could use you for a little plan I cooked up." He checked on Louis again and lowered his voice to a whisper. "I was gonna get these names, see, and set up a little business for myself with the help of a friend in Trenton. Maybe fill out some credit applications, or make some fake ID's. Tom happened to mention once that you were an expert at forging names."

Grace got a cold, hollow feeling in the pit of her stomach. She couldn't believe she was hearing this. The cabbage she was cutting suddenly looked an awful lot like Tom's head. She gave it a solid whack with the knife.

"So what you're telling me is that you met Tom at a car show, and he started off the conversation by telling you I have a record for forgery and ID theft?"

"Nah. Nothing like that. We didn't have that conversation until after..."

"After what?"

Nick stopped chopping. "What are you so shocked about? Like I said last night, did you think it was a coincidence that we hooked up at the club?"

"But *I* came to *you*. On a dare."

He raised his eyebrows. "Okay. Think about this. There were a hundred guys at that club. Why'd you come to me?"

"Because…"

Because you are so much sexier than Ludmilla. Because your eyes make me want to do things that might be a teensy bit illegal. Because I was feeling obsolete, and you made me feel like a teenager again.

"…Because you were looking at me." Realization hit her like a softball to the head. "You knew if I saw you looking at me, I'd come over."

Damn. It had all been a setup.

Her throat tightened. She chopped unmercifully at the cabbage. *Die. Die!*

"How did you know I'd be there?" she asked.

Nick shrugged. "I followed you from your house."

"You know where I live?" She took a deep breath. "Then why didn't you just come to the house to get the damned computer key this morning?"

"I did, but you were gone already."

Chop, chop, chop.

"Hey." Nick gently removed the knife from her hands and took her by the shoulders, turning her to face him. "I was looking at you because I wanted you to come over. But I kissed you because I couldn't help myself."

She couldn't move. The combination of Nick's beautiful hands on her, his gorgeous eyes staring into hers and the smell of food drove her over the edge.

"Kiss me one more time," she said, and closed her eyes.

CHAPTER 11.5

Sunday, 5:45 a.m.
Taking a Dive

Pete pressed the buzzer screwed onto the check-in desk at the Sleep-In Motel, three miles from the Boise airport on Interstate 85.

He'd checked the room Balboa had said Morton was in, but it was empty, the open curtains revealing no sign of occupancy. He wasn't surprised.

Pete yawned. He would have liked nothing better than to check into one of these rooms, as skeevy as it might be, and sleep for ten hours. But he wasn't there to sleep. He was geek hunting.

The night manager staggered out of the room behind the desk in a bathrobe that looked like it hadn't been washed since...well, ever. His hair stuck up on one side at a ninety-degree angle.

"Hey, Gumby. Where's Pokey?" Pete said.

The manager gave him a blank look. "Help you?"

"Yeah. I'm looking for someone." He pulled a grainy picture of Morton out of his pocket.

The manager shook his head without even looking at the picture.

"His mother's been in an accident. I need to find him."

"I can't help you, sir. Our guest register is confidential."

"Why? Is the President staying here?"

The night manager shook his head and again turned to go back to his room.

Pete pulled a crisp fifty out of his wallet and snapped it. "Hey. I've got a president right here. President Ulysses S. Grant. Can he check in?"

Gumby rubbed the back of his neck, and turned around. "Okay. Let me have a look at the picture." He stuffed the fifty into the pocket of his robe, and held the photo of Morton up to the light.

"Uh-huh. This guy checked in a couple of days ago. With a girl."

"He still here?"

"Nope. Only stayed one night."

Which proved Morton had had no intention of waiting around for Nick to deliver the key to Skobelov, and for Skobelov to Fed Ex him a check for the goods. He knew there'd be no check for an empty key.

"How'd he pay?" Pete asked.

"Credit card, I think."

Oh, the irony. "Can you look it up for me?"

The manager flashed him a look of annoyance. "Come on, man. I'm tired."

Pete slid a twenty onto the counter. "Here. Andrew Jackson wants to check in, too."

Gumby powered on the old computer behind the desk. The hard disk whined and clicked as he tapped on the keys. Eventually, the printer behind him spat out a sheet of paper. He tore it off, gave it a quick look and handed it to Pete. "Can I go back to bed, now?"

"Just one more thing. Where does the trash from the rooms end up?"

"In the Dumpster behind room sixteen."

"Has it been taken away in the last two days?"

"No. Pickup is Monday and Thursday mornings. Your guy checked out Friday."

"Mind if I take a look?"

"In the trash? Knock yourself out."

Pete located room sixteen with little problem. The Sleep-In was laid out like a horseshoe that started with the office and ended at a maintenance unit across the wide driveway. The rooms were numbered one to twenty-six, excluding thirteen. He guessed anyone unfortunate enough to have to stay at this dump already had all the bad luck they could handle.

Room sixteen was located on the curve of the horse-shoe, next to a narrow alley containing vending machines and an ice maker. The alley led through to the back of the building, where the Dumpster stood beside an access road off the main highway. A regular rodent fast-food drive-through.

Pete shinnied up the side and peered in. The Dumpster was nearly full.

"Great. Just great."

He climbed into the Dumpster and poked through a few bags, soon realizing he was going to have to dig deeper. He covered his face with the collar of his coat, and worked his way down through the refuse.

How did Ferret do this for a living? A professional Dumpster diver—a guy who dug information on individuals and businesses out of the trash—Ferret spent the majority of his nights knee-deep in other people's Chinese takeout, used tissues and liquefied vegetables.

It was definitely freaking Pete out.

He hacked down through the refuse, ripping open dozens of large trash bags until he found one that contained a bunch of smaller bags—the kind that lined little motel room trash cans.

He began ripping them open, like small piñatas filled

with delightful prizes. Beer cans. Coke cans. Tissues. CornNut wrappers. Half-eaten donuts. And—

Pete gave an involuntary shudder—

Used condoms.

He was about to give up when he struck pay dirt.

A Sleep-In notepad with several phone numbers starting with a 215 area code. Southeast Pennsylvania. And a 609 area code. Central New Jersey.

In the same bag he found a list of airlines and flight times, and it didn't take an agent's intuition to guess where the flights were landing.

Morton was playing games. And he was playing them right in Pete's backyard.

Pete pocketed his treasures and climbed out of the Dumpster, picking a crumpled Band-Aid off of his shoe.

He flicked open his cell phone.

"United Air Lines. How can I help you?" The voice on the other end of the line was annoyingly chipper for—he looked at his watch—six-fifteen in the morning.

"I need to get on the next flight to Philadelphia."

CHAPTER 12

Sunday, 6:50 a.m.
Kulebiaka and Bad Boys

By the time breakfast rolled around, Grace had worked up a pretty good appetite chopping and trying to quell the sexual tension that had built up between her and Nick.

Louis awoke refreshed from his nap, and Grace served up a huge platter of flaky pastries filled with eggs, meat, cabbage and rice.

"What is this stuff?" Nick asked, through a mouthful of food.

"*Kulebiaka*. It's an Eastern European dish."

"Where'd you learn to cook like this?"

Grace finished off her third glass of wine, ignoring the little voice that told her she'd pay for this tomorrow. Or rather, later today. "An executive at Tom's company was Russian. I took lessons so I could have him and his wife over for dinner. Impress them."

"*Mmmph.*" Louis bent over his plate like a vulture protecting a zebra carcass.

"You did all that for your husband?" said Nick.

"It was important to him."

"Was it important to you?"

Grace thought about that.

She supposed it was important, at the time. Very important. Her whole life had revolved around the ability to make a good impression. To make Tom happy.

But looking back on things now, she wished she hadn't been so obsessed with making everything perfect. She wished she would have had more fun, like she did in her life before marriage.

She said, "Tom was important to me. And my kids were. *Are*. They're the most important."

"But what do *you* want, Grace? For yourself?" Nick's heavy-lidded gaze felt like a thousand tiny fingers on her skin. She turned away, not wanting him to see her blush.

She'd been asking herself that very question for months, now.

"I don't know." She stood and began clearing the plates.

"Don't worry about that," Nick said. "Lou will get the dishes."

Louis grunted again.

Nick poured her another glass of wine and took her arm, leading her into the small living room, where he sat beside her on the sofa.

Close.

Too close.

She edged away and took a swig of wine.

Nick reached out and twirled a piece of her hair in his fingers. "I like you, Grace. Even though you're not my type."

"So I've been told." Grace tried to breathe slowly. She recited her mantra in her head. *Namu Amida Butsu. Namu Amida Butsu.*

Despite the fact that being with Nick would be wrong on so many levels, Grace's heartbeat quickened. It was like the time in high school when she had gone beneath the bleachers at a football game to look for the pencil she'd dropped—the one with a troll doll on the top. Bobby Gaither was already down there, leaning up against one of the metal supports, smoking a cigarette. He had looked so cool in his Members Only jacket, with his hair hanging over dark, dark eyes.

"Come here," he'd said. And because she hadn't wanted to look chicken, she'd gone over.

"You want a cigarette?" He'd held out a pack of Newports. And because she hadn't wanted to look dorky, she'd said yes.

It was the first cigarette she'd ever smoked. She'd coughed a little bit and her eyes had watered, and when she had finished she'd been light-headed and had felt like she might throw up. It was a feeling she'd have around men many times to come.

"You wanna make out?" Bobby had asked. And because she hadn't wanted to look like a goody-goody, she'd complied.

The ground had lurched, and above her the bleachers had spun like they were caught in a tornado. Bobby's tongue had slid over hers, tasting of cigarettes and Pop Rocks from the concession stand.

She'd felt bad, and wild, and her lips had burned deliciously. She'd forgotten all about the troll pencil. She'd gone below the bleachers a girl, and had returned a woman. Or, almost a woman. She was changed.

That Monday, Bobby had lied to all the boys in wood shop that he'd gone to second base with her. She hadn't bothered to deny it. Those few, carefree minutes when she hadn't thought of anything else but the way she'd been feeling with Bobby had been worth the smudge on her reputation.

Nick moved closer to her on the sofa, and she realized she could have that again. Right now. A few transcendent minutes in the arms of a bad, bad boy.

He leaned in and kissed her, and she felt herself letting go.

She pulled away. "I'm going to bed now."

Nick grinned. He stood when she did, but she shook her head.

She realized she'd had just about enough of bad boys.

"Let me clarify," she said. "I'm going to bed now. Alone."

Sunday, 2:29 p.m.
Primates

Grace woke up drooling on a strange pillow, in a room decorated with subdued animal patterns and framed prints of African savannahs in gold-gilt frames.

She was sprawled on a bed in her underwear, her sweatshirt and yoga pants lying in a heap beside the bed. Downstairs, she could hear the sound of men arguing.

She looked at her watch and realized Kevin would be finishing up his soccer tournament about now.

She pulled on her clothes, combed her hair with her fingers and marched downstairs to the living room, where Pete and Nick were facing off against each other like a pair of apes in the wild, posturing and beating their chests.

Pete looked wiped out. "Didn't you even bother to check the damned key before you took it from Morton?" he snapped.

"Hell, yes. What do you think I am? Stupid?"

"You said it, not me."

"I told you, I checked the damned key. The names, the social security numbers, they were all there."

"Then what the hell happened?"

Nick rubbed the stubble on his chin. "I don't know. Maybe he switched it with another key or something before I left."

"Well, did you give him an opportunity to do that? Did you leave him alone with the key?"

"No." But Nick's face flushed.

"What?" said Pete.

"I don't know. Maybe…" He sighed.

"What happened?" said Pete.

"There was a girl in the room with Morton. Great hair, long legs. Stacked." Nick lit a cigarette. "She followed me into the bathroom, and one thing led to another…"

Pete gave Grace a sympathetic look.

"What?" she said. "I don't care what he does."

Pete turned back to Nick. "And then what? You did her in the bathroom?"

"Nah. Nothing like that. We just fooled around a little."

"And during that time, Morton was alone with the key?"

"Well, yeah. But how would I know he'd pull something funny? He was there to sell me the damn thing. Why would he tamper with it?"

Pete flopped down into a chair. "I don't know."

Nick crushed out his cigarette in an ashtray on the coffee table. "Now what? I told Viktor I'd have the names for him by tonight."

"Well, you won't. Even if we could set up a fake key, it would take time." Pete buried his face in his hands. "Shit."

Louis came in the room. "Fegley wants you to call him, Pete."

"Of course he does."

"Who's Fegley?" said Grace.

"My boss." Pete pulled his cell phone out of his pocket. "I guess I'll have to tell him we're done. Finished. I'll have him set Balboa up in witness protection, and we'll pull out."

"Ho, hey." Nick snatched the phone from Pete. "Not so fast."

"Listen," Pete said. "I know you're not thrilled with the prospect of entering the program, but you're my only chance of making a case against Skobelov. I won't have much now, but if I can't get anything on him at all, I've wasted two years. And I can't risk you getting popped or taking off on me before I have the chance to build the case."

Nick held his arms out. "I wouldn't take off on you."

"I'm supposed to take your word after what you pulled Friday? You'd screw me in a heartbeat."

Nick grinned. "Nah. You're not my type."

Pete grabbed his cell phone back from Nick.

Nick drummed his fingers on the coffee table. "Maybe I could make it up to you."

Pete shook his head. "It's over."

"What if I could buy some more time? Another day or two? Just enough time for you to find Morton or put something else together."

Pete was quiet for a while. "How?"

Nick jerked his head at Grace. "Her."

Grace sat up straight. "Me? What about me?"

"What about her?" Pete said.

"Her cooking." Nick stood up and began to pace behind the sofa. "The only thing the Russian loves more than money is food. He's always complaining he can't get a decent Russian meal in Philadelphia." He pointed at Grace. "She can give it to him."

Louis nodded. "She's good, Pete."

"What, that hamburger stuff?"

"Nah," said Lou. "That was bush-league. She's been making some great food here. You missed it while you were out in Boise."

"Viktor would do anything for good borscht," Nick said, his voice rising with excitement. "He'd definitely give us more time."

"Uh-uh. No way," Pete said.

"No way," Grace agreed. Her arms broke out in goose-flesh just remembering Skobelov's evil laugh.

"See?" Pete said. "She's just a suburban housewife. She's not up for something like that."

A tiny spark flared in the back of Grace's brain. "Excuse me? How do you know what I'm up for?"

She knew it was crazy, but them were fightin' words.

As "just a suburban housewife," she'd battled forty-one hours of childbirth labor, months of colic, years of poopy diapers, endless nights of croup, homework, broken hearts and broken bones.

She'd cooked, cleaned, finessed, flattered, cajoled, faked orgasms, faked joy over crappy anniversary gifts and faked holding it all together when Tom walked out on them.

Surely, she could survive cooking for one maniacal Russian mobster for a day or two.

Despite earlier vows to go back to her mundane life, she discovered she really *did* want to do this. Her inner Charlie's Angel begged to be free.

"I'd be there," Nick argued. "I'd protect her."

Pete snorted. "Right."

But Grace could tell by the look in his eye that he might at least consider the idea.

She touched his arm. "I want to do it."

CHAPTER 12.5

Sunday, 3:22 p.m.
Salvage Work

Grace was clearly out of her mind.

The Russian was volatile. Dangerous. Three hundred pounds of menacing flesh.

If she were tougher, more familiar with the underworld, he might consider it. But it had become clear to him that what Grace had been saying all along was true. She really wasn't Nick's girlfriend.

He knew, because there wasn't a woman alive who could hear her boyfriend confess to making out in a sleazy motel bathroom with another woman and not bat an eyelash. If he knew nothing else about women, he knew that.

He still wasn't completely sure she had nothing to do

with this case—he couldn't completely ignore her record, after all. But putting her in close quarters with Skobelov?

He couldn't do it.

He looked down at her hand, so pale and fragile looking, resting on his arm. Her touch was gentle, and he felt a surge of uncharacteristic protectiveness.

Damn. What was he getting all sappy about? She was the one offering to put her neck on the line. She knew what she was getting into, and if she could possibly save his case, why shouldn't he take her up on the offer?

Grace and Nick and Lou looked at him like they were waiting for him to sing something from *Yentl* or start spinning plates on broomsticks.

His cell phone buzzed in his hand. He looked down at the number.

Fegley. Crap.

He took a deep breath and flipped open his phone. "Fegley? Hey, there might be a way to salvage this thing after all."

CHAPTER 13

Sunday, 4:40 p.m.
Tangled Up

Pete followed her through the front door of her house, into the foyer.

"Nice place. How long have you lived here?"

"Fourteen years. My ex-husband inherited it from his aunt. When we got it, it was just about falling down, so we had our work cut out for us."

He strolled into the living room, hands behind his back, peering at everything as if he were a detective in an old-fashioned mystery. He pointed to the walk-in fireplace. "Is the cartouche original?"

"Most of it. But a few of the pieces had to be recreated." The fleur-de-lis shield beneath the mantel had been a pet project of hers. It had taken weeks of research and phone calls to find the perfect craftsmen to handle the restoration. But it had been worth it. In Grace's opinion, the cartouche was the heart of the house. She'd remodeled the entire interior around that design.

Pete strolled to the cabinet in the corner. "Nice étagère."

What was this guy, gay? Nobody knew what an étagère was, except for interior designers and gay men.

"Tom always called it the junk cabinet. He can't stand knickknacks."

"Those are hardly knickknacks. I see some Lladró there. Royal Copenhagen. And is that Lalique?"

Definitely gay.

"Do you collect figurines?" she asked.

Red crept up from beneath his collar like the liquid in a thermometer, turning his entire face the mottled color of a bruised apple. "My mother does. I get her one every Christmas."

"So how do you know so much about the other stuff? Cartouches and étagères?"

"My sister's an interior decorator. I guess I just picked up some of the terminology."

Grace was inexplicably relieved that he wasn't gay. "Did your sister decorate your house in Philadelphia?"

If possible, his face grew even redder. "No. I decorated it myself. I guess I picked up a little more than terminology." He cleared his throat. "Are you gonna go pack some clothes, or what?"

"Do I have time to take a quick shower?"

He looked at his watch. "Make it fast."

"There are drinks in the fridge if you want something." She ran up the steps, avoiding the squeaky one, the third from the top, out of habit.

Her bedroom was at the end of the hall, through ivory-painted French doors. She and Tom had combined two smaller bedrooms to create a modestly sized but luxurious master suite with a fireplace at either end; a large bathroom with a claw-foot spa tub, shower and double sink; and a huge walk-in closet and dressing area.

It was the one part of the house that didn't have an authentic colonial feel. But she was addicted to long, hot baths, and she had a lot of clothes and shoes, things that weren't exactly priorities in colonial times.

She locked the door to the bathroom and stripped off the dirty yoga pants and sweatshirt. She hadn't showered or used deodorant in nearly three days—a bodily state unknown to her since her brief membership in an environmental group her freshman year in college.

She and a bunch of fellow EarthSavers had camped out with video cameras in the woods next to a fertilizer plant to prove phosphate chemicals were being dumped into a nearby stream. But instead of nailing corporate

America, the trip had pretty much turned into an excuse to drink a lot of beer and nail each other.

She'd left pretty quickly, since she really had no desire to make naughty videos with people who hadn't showered or brushed their teeth in several days.

Now, she showered in record time, then attempted to blow-dry her new coif with the round-bristled brush Tammy had given her. Halfway through, the brush got hopelessly tangled in her hair. She turned off the dryer and cursed the time-sucking style.

She could only hope it would turn out to be her biggest regret of the weekend.

Pete called to her from downstairs.

"Gimme five minutes!" she yelled.

She sprinted from the bathroom to her closet, where she dug through a drawer full of "functional" undergarments until she found a pair of underwear and a matching bra. Tom's idea of a nice Mother's Day gift.

She leafed through the hangers, picking out a pair of black Liz Claiborne pants and a pink, loose-weave sweater. She had the sweater halfway over her head when she heard the squeaky step and realized that Pete was upstairs. And that she'd left the door to her bedroom open.

"I'll be right out!" She tried to pull the sweater on, but it got stuck halfway over her head.

The brush! The brush was still tangled in her hair!

She bent over and clawed at the sweater, which only became more and more snarled in the brush the harder she tried to get it off.

"Grace?" Pete's voice came from inside her bedroom.

Pleasepleaseplease. Don't let him see me like this.

Why? What do you care?

I don't.

Yes, you do. And you were just kissing Nick last night.

So what? I can kiss whomever I want.

Slut.

Prude.

Hey. Both of you. You do realize you're talking to yourself.

"Grace?"

"Don't come in!"

A warm hand touched the small of her back. "Too late. Can I help you?"

"No!" She wrestled with the sweater some more but only succeeded in getting out of breath. She stood up and peered out at him through an armhole.

One side of Pete's mouth was curled up into a smirk. "Let me get it. There's a piece of wood sticking out through the sweater."

Pete worked the sweater over her head, leaving her standing there in her closet in nothing but her underwear. Why, oh, why couldn't she have worn a camisole to cover the road map of stretch marks across her belly?

Luckily, there was something to distract Pete.

"What's that thing in your hair?" he said.

"A hairbrush."

"Mmm. Are you just going to leave it there?"

"Yes. It's an accessory." She pulled on her pants. "What are you doing in my bedroom?"

"Your phone was ringing. Someone left you a message, and it sounded like it might be important."

"You listened to my message?"

"I couldn't help it. I was sitting right next to the answering machine."

"Get out."

"Hurry up."

She pushed Pete out of the closet and slammed the door.

"You *were* kidding about the hairbrush, weren't you?" he said from the other side.

Sunday, 5:23 p.m.
Feeding Dracula

By the time she came back downstairs, Pete was sitting on the sofa leafing through her wedding album.

"Where did you get that?"

"On the bookshelf over there. Behind *Divorce for Dummies* and *A Hundred Healthy Ways to Channel Your Rage.* Who's the guy in the tux?"

"That would be my husband."

"You mean your ex-husband."

"He wasn't my ex-husband at the time, obviously."

"You didn't look very happy on your wedding day."

"Yeah, well. I had PMS."

"Must have been a fun honeymoon."

She snatched the book from his lap. "Are you ready?"

"What about your message?"

"Right." She stuffed the wedding album under the sofa, and went over to the answering machine on the mahogany console table.

Three messages.

The first was from Kevin. "Hi, Mom. Grandma said your cell phone wasn't working. Guess what? We won! Dad took us out for pizza after. Don't forget to feed Dracula. Bye."

Oh, crap. She'd forgotten about Dracula. She hit the pause button.

"Dracula?" said Pete.

"Kevin's frog. I was supposed to pick up some crickets at the pet store yesterday."

"You want me to go check on the frog? I mean, just in case he's…"

"Okay. That would be good. If he *is*… you know, there's a shoe box under Kevin's bed. If he's not, there's a container up there that might have a few crickets left in it. Just put them in the frog's tank."

"Where's Kevin's room?"

"Up the stairs, make a left, second door on the right."

Pete headed for Kevin's room, and she unpaused the answering machine.

The second message was from Lorraine. "Grace. How *are* you? I'm calling to remind you that you're up next to host cards. I know things are hard for you right now. Call me if you need a friend, okay?"

Sure. Will do. Because I'd like my business broadcast to every woman in South Whitpain in the eighteen to forty-five demographic.

Third message. "Grace? Pick up, Gracie." Tom's perfect diction streamed out from the machine. "Did you sign those papers yet? I really, really need them. Call me as soon as you get this."

She punched the erase button, wishing there was a button big enough to erase Tom himself.

CHAPTER 13.5

Sunday, 5:32 p.m.
Three-hour Tour

Pete listened to Grace play the message he'd just heard come in, wondering who the guy with the Cary Grant voice was. Her ex-husband, probably. Didn't she say he called her Gracie?

He felt a twinge of something low in his gut that felt suspiciously like jealousy. Her ex was a good-looking guy. An all-star quarterback type. Prom king. Class president. At least, that's the way he looked in the wedding pictures.

But hey, a lot could change in fourteen years. He could have gained fifty pounds. Come down with some horrible skin disease. Lost his hair.

Pete raked his fingers through his own dark red mop. At least he didn't have to worry about *that* anytime soon.

He sucked in his stomach and walked into the living room. "Good news. The frog's still kicking. You ready to go?"

Grace spun around, wiping a tear from her cheek.

No. No, no, no. No tears. "You okay?"

"Yeah. I just miss my kids."

"Hey, listen." He touched her arm. "You don't have to do this."

She shook her head. "No. I want to."

"I'm gonna warn you again. Skobelov is a dangerous man."

"But you'll be listening in, right? You'll have Nick wired. And all I'm going to do is cook for him."

"You could get caught in the middle of something."

She smiled. "I'll be careful."

"Good." And the next thing he knew, he was kissing her.

It started as hardly more than a peck, the kind of kiss he might give his sister. But the heat hit him like a nuclear blast, and soon he pulled her closer, losing himself in the taste of her lips. The flowery scent of her shampoo.

She melted against him and made little kitten sounds.

And then, as if she'd suddenly found herself embracing a tiger, she backed slowly out of his arms.

"Well."

"Grace, I'm sorry. I shouldn't have done that. It was completely inappropriate."

"No. No problem. We should go."

Damn. He screwed up. "Grace—"

"Pete, it's okay. It wasn't just you. It was me, too." She pushed the hair out of her eyes. "Will you help me with my bag?"

A big blue duffel sat near the door. He got a hernia just picking it up.

"What the— What's in this thing?"

She shrugged. "I didn't know what to pack. I mean, what does one wear to cook *rasstegai* for a Russian mobster?"

"You're only going to be there a day. Maybe two."

"I can't help it. It's Three-hour Tour Syndrome."

"What?"

"Like on 'Gilligan's Island.' Three-hour Tour Syndrome. They brought enough clothes for several months, even though they were only supposed to be going on a three-hour boat cruise."

"Yeah, but the Skipper and Gilligan only had one set of clothes."

"That's why I never dated a sailor."

He hefted the duffel over his shoulder. "You're an interesting woman, Grace Becker."

CHAPTER 14

Sunday, 6:10 p.m.
Channeling Nancy Drew

As Pete's Taurus sped toward Philadelphia, Grace couldn't help but think about how different things were—how different *she* was—less than forty-eight hours ago.

She'd been picked up by a Secret Service agent, had hung out at a strip club, had been recruited to cook for a Russian mobster and had kissed two different men—two very different men—all in two days' time.

If only Cecilia and Dannie and Roseanna could see her now. This was turning out to be an unbelievable game of truth or dare.

In fact, she's begun to look at it all like a test. A measure of her ability to change and adapt. She would definitely need it in the days and weeks to come, as she tried to put her life back together.

She switched on the radio. The easy-listening station filtered out from the speakers. She gave Pete a sad, knowing look. "Mind if I change the station?"

"Go ahead."

She flipped through until she heard Elvis Costello singing "Radio Radio."

Pete drummed on the steering wheel.

He had nice hands. Long, straight fingers with just a few freckles. No knobby joints, hairy knuckles or chewed nails.

The rest of him wasn't bad, either. He had a sprinkling of freckles across his nose and the beginnings of a ginger-colored five o'clock shadow.

While Nick was Death by Chocolate, Pete was a cinnamon bun.

And she was developing quite an appetite.

She rolled down the window and let the wind ruffle her new, short haircut. She hadn't felt this wild, this free, since her college days. She, Grace Poleiski, was going to help the Secret Service crack a case.

"Uh-oh," Pete said.

"What?"

"I recognize that look."

"What look?"

"That Nancy Drew, Girl Detective look."

She looked out the window. "Don't be ridiculous. I was a Hardy Boys fan."

"When you get in there," Pete said, "I want you to keep your mouth shut. You're there to cook. This isn't amateur night at the detective agency."

"I get it."

Pete switched off the radio. "I mean it, Grace. The best thing you can do for this case is to leave everything up to Nick."

"I can't even believe you can say those words with a straight face." She stared out the window.

Pete took the next exit and pulled over onto the side of the road. "Look. I know Nick isn't the most reliable informant, but he's all I've got. You're not going to help me by sticking your neck out, and possibly putting an already nervous perpetrator on alert. And I don't want to have to worry about you."

He'd worry about her?

She rolled this around in her mind for a moment, just to see how she felt about it. It had been a long time since anyone, including Tom, had worried about her. Besides her mother, that is.

She smiled. "I'll behave. I promise."

"Good."

They drove to a vacant lot on the border of West Philadelphia. Broken glass glittered under the streetlight like diamonds on black velvet, and plastic trash bags danced across the space, only to be trapped up against a sagging chain-link fence. Tufts of straggly weeds growing up through the cracks in the macadam offered proof that surviving in this part of town wasn't impossible, it just took persistence.

Pete put the car in Park but left it running for the heat. They sat listening to the radio in comfortable silence.

A few minutes later, Lou and Nick pulled up in front of them in a baby-blue and white 1959 Buick LeSabre with miles of fin and chrome.

"Wow," Grace said. "Nice car."

Pete grunted, and opened the car door. "Come on."

He swung around the back of the Taurus to get Grace's duffel bag out of the trunk, while she went over to admire the LeSabre.

Louis sat in the car talking on his cell phone, but Nick got out and came around, patting the roof of the Buick.

Grace ran her hand over chrome on the massive fin in the back. "Beautiful."

"You like classic cars?" Nick asked.

"I learned to appreciate them. I went to a lot of car shows with Tom. He has a '76 Corvette."

"Yeah. I know."

Grace looked up at him. "I guess you would."

Nick stuffed his hands in the pockets of his leather jacket and shrugged.

"Did you ever show the car?" she asked.

"A couple times. But I don't like other people touching my girl."

Grace snatched her hand off the fin.

Nick laughed. "It's okay. I don't mind if you do."

Louis got out of the car. "Okay. You ready?"

Nick nodded. He looked at Grace. "How about you?"

"I'm ready."

Pete came over to the car with Grace's bag, and Nick opened the trunk.

"Remember," Pete said to Nick. "Try to get him to talk about his various business ventures, especially the identification fraud. And if anything goes wrong, you know the code word?"

"Pineapple."

"Right. Just say *pineapple* and we'll be there, with an army of cops. Don't take any chances." Pete looked at Grace. "No chances."

"Got it," Nick said.

"Don't screw me over, Nick. This is your last chance."

"Yeah, yeah." Nick threw the bag in the trunk and slammed it shut with the kind of sonorous *kathunk* only a 1950s Buick could make.

Grace sensed some tension beneath Nick's bravado. She wondered how he'd gotten involved in all of this in the first place, and what his expectations had been.

Then again, she was a fine one to talk when she didn't even know what her own expectations should be.

Sunday, 6:32 p.m.
Feminine Protection

A few minutes later, Grace and Nick drove up in front of an old, run-down brick building less than half a block from the railroad tracks. The place looked as if it might have housed some sort of manufacturing plant.

"Feminine products," Nick said.

"What?"

"It was a feminine products plant." He got out and came around to open her door.

"Like a tampon factory?"

The tips of his ears turned red, and he shrugged. "I guess so. Jeez."

She almost laughed. Here was a man who wasn't bothered by guns or Secret Service agents or crazy Russians, but the word *tampon* could kill him with embarrassment.

Pete should have made that his secret word instead of *pineapple*.

"What are we doing here?" she said.

"You'll see." They walked toward a door beside a fenced-off parking lot littered with potholes and pigeon droppings.

Grace's stomach fluttered. Not the good kind of

flutter, like when you get the first three out of five numbers on lotto or when you see an old boyfriend at a class reunion. It was the bad kind of flutter, like when the phone rings at three in the morning or when the doctor leaves a message on your machine saying he wants to discuss the results of your STD test.

"What about my stuff?" Grace said. "This doesn't exactly seem like the safest of areas. I'd rather not leave it in the car. And come to think of it, you might not want to leave your *car*."

"Don't worry. There are people watching."

She breathed deeply, and tried to calm herself with the thought that Pete was listening in on everything. She wondered what would happen if *she* shouted the word *pineapple*. Would Pete and Louis rush to her rescue, too? Or would she just look like a lunatic shouting "pineapple" at Nick's chest?

Nick took her hand and gave it a squeeze. "Don't worry, babe. I'm right here. I'll protect you."

That wasn't as comforting a thought as she'd have liked.

He pressed a small, lit doorbell beside a big, glass door. A buzzer sounded, and Nick pushed open the door and led her into the lobby of the tampon plant.

A brick wall with handlebar mustache and a pit-bull scowl sat behind a semicircular receptionist's desk, watching football on a small television. Behind him

Grace could make out the shadow of the word *Femm-Care* where the letters had been removed from the wall.

"Hey, Benny. Who's winning?" Nick said.

"Stinking Giants."

"Damn. I got a nickel on the Eagles."

Benny grunted and pressed a button on the desk. A dark brown elevator door opened on the other side of the lobby.

Nick dragged Grace into the elevator and punched Four, the highest floor on the panel.

"Why are we here?" she whispered. "It looks abandoned."

Nick shook his head and looked up at the corner of the elevator, where a security camera stared back at her.

The elevator grunted and wheezed and finally ground to a halt on the fourth floor. The lit button went out with a ding that sounded like a bad note struck on a toddler's xylophone.

The door opened, and Grace stifled a gasp. Not a tampon in sight.

Instead, she and Nick stepped off the elevator into a gorgeous entrance hall with a parquet floor and a lush fresh-flower arrangement on a marble credenza that stood taller than her.

To the left were two white doors trimmed in gold. They reminded her of doors that might lead to a French courtier's boudoir.

"I get the feeling we're not in Femm-Care anymore, Toto," she said.

Nick smiled. "The plant is pretty much empty, except for this. This is Skobelov's apartment. It's modeled after the Emperor's Suite at Caesars Palace in Las Vegas. Look." He pointed to the ceiling.

A reproduction of Michelangelo's *The Creation of Adam* was painted on the ceiling.

"What do you think?"

"Unbelievable."

Nick slung his arm over her shoulders. "You ready?"

She nodded.

He knocked on the door.

A woman in black stretch pants and a leopard-skin tank top opened the door. Her strawberry blond hair turned under just before it touched her shoulders, and spiky bangs brushed the tops of her penciled eyebrows.

The arch of those eyebrows gave the woman an innocent expression, and if it weren't for the cynical set of her lips, Grace might have thought she'd been kidnapped and stuffed into these clothes for some sort of bizarre episode of *Candid Camera*.

"Hey, Tina. The Russian here?"

"Where else would he be? He has a nickel on the Eagles, so he's in a rotten mood."

"Hey, this is my girlfriend, Grace."

Tina's gaze ran from Grace's hair to her toes and back. "Oh, yeah? She looks a little uptight for you, Nicky."

"You think? She's kind of a surprise for Viktor."

"Oh, yeah?" She put a hand on the curve of her hip.

"Not *that* kind of surprise," Grace said quickly.

Tina shrugged. "He's in the TV room." She drifted away, her high heels clicking on the marble floor.

Grace followed Nick into the apartment. The marble floor gave way to gold and black carpet in a living room dominated by a buttery leather sectional couch. Heavy gold drapes hid the functional factory windows, while a stunning crystal chandelier in the middle of the high ceiling gave the room a soft glow.

A seventy-two-inch flat-screen plasma television hung on a distant wall, broadcasting the Eagles-Giants game in digital splendor. The players looked so crisp, so real, Grace felt as if she could reach out and pinch their butts while they huddled up.

In contrast to the players, the man who watched the game hardly seemed real at all.

Viktor Skobelov was a cross between Jabba the Hutt and Chewbacca. A fat, furry, noxious blob, spread out like molasses along the length of the sectional. Grace wouldn't have been at all surprised to see Princess Leia in a gold bikini chained to the coffee table.

The Russian let out a belch and hit the mute button

195

on the TV. "You have something for me, Nicky? I am not in good mood."

His words seemed like an effort. Slurred. Yakov Smirnoff on Quaaludes.

Grace might have laughed if she hadn't been so terrified. She had to pee, but she knew it was an inopportune moment.

"I don't have the names just yet," Nick said.

The Russian shook his head. "I am not happy, Nicky. What we going to do?"

"I'm working on it."

"You say that yesterday."

"I know, I know. I'm getting close. But in the meantime, I brought you something else. A gift. Something to keep you happy while I get the names." Nick dragged Grace in front of him like a human shield. "This is my girlfriend, Grace."

The Russian's tiny eyes raked over her like he was inspecting a side of beef. She gave an involuntary shiver.

"What you do?" he said.

She stared dumbly at him, mesmerized by the trembling of his jowls.

"What you do?" he repeated. "You do leather? Rubber?" He looked at Nick. "She's a little old."

Old?

Grace opened her mouth to inform the fat bastard that

she wouldn't touch him with somebody *else's* hands let alone her own. But Nick gave her arm a hard squeeze before she could get the words out.

"No, no. She's not that kind of gift," Nick said quickly. "She cooks."

"She cooks? What? That freaking noodles and tomatoes you call food?"

Nick grinned. "Nope. Eastern European cuisine."

The Russian's eyebrows shot up. "Like what?"

"*Kulebiaka. Borscht. Kulich. Rasstegai. Okroshka,*" Grace answered.

The Russian leaned back on the couch and trained his gaze on her as if were so hungry he might devour her words. Or maybe her.

Her toes curled, and not in a good way, but she met his gaze without blinking.

"You better hope she good, Nicky," Skobelov said. "Real good. If not, you are dead man."

CHAPTER 14.5

Sunday, 7:02 p.m.
Happy Noodle

Pete checked his watch for the eightieth time. He picked up his cell phone and hit the speed dial for Lou's number.

"Yo."

"Any sign of Morton?"

"Not yet. But lots of party girls walking around this part of town. Christ, who dresses these ladies?"

"Lou, you're so friggin' interested in women's clothes, you should be a designer. You could create a whole line of clothes just for hookers and strippers."

"*Hmp.*" Lou sounded as if he might actually consider that career change.

"Let me know when Morton and the girl show up."

"Right." Louis hung up.

While Pete listened in on Nick and Grace, Louis was staking out the hotel that matched the phone number Pete had found in the Dumpster in Boise. It had turned out to be a low-rent establishment in Northeast Philly that was one step away from renting rooms by the hour.

The desk clerk confirmed that Morton had checked in the day before with a cute little brunette in tow but they hadn't been around much.

Pete figured the girl for the one Nick had groped in the bathroom of the Sleep-In.

He wondered how the two had been spending their time. Checking out the Liberty Bell? Maybe the Betsy Ross House? He doubted it.

He adjusted the frequency on the receivers for Balboa's body wire.

Damn. Balboa and Grace had separated. Grace had left the living room and Nick. Pete could hear only the football game—he had a nickel on the Eagles—and Balboa's incessant humming, which Pete suspected was a calculated effort to make him crazy.

He wondered if he shouldn't have put a wire on Grace, too, just in case.

The thought of her trapped in a room with Skobelov or that gorilla he called a bodyguard made Pete sick.

His cell phone launched into Wild Cherry's "Play That Funky Music," and he flipped it open. "Yeah?"

"Morton's here with the girl. Just went upstairs with a bag of takeout from Happy Noodle."

"Good. Let's try to get a bug in there. Let me know if he goes anywhere."

Pete flipped the phone shut and propped his feet up on the dash, just as the announcer signed off on the football game.

Stinking Giants.

CHAPTER 15

Sunday, 8:18 p.m.
Wild One

The Russian's kitchen was a cook's nirvana, with a Viking stove, Sub-Zero refrigerator, granite countertops, Judge cookware and a spice rack that included obscure spices sold only by men in trench coats in the alleys of Chinatown.

Unlike Pete's bare refrigerator, Skobelov's was stocked with everything imaginable, from Caviar to cottage cheese.

The SieMatic cabinets held seven different kinds of rice, four kinds of flour, six kinds of honey and a bag of dried something called Hu-Hu that she suspected might be related to the insect family.

And for her listening pleasure, there was even a Bose Wave system mounted beneath one of the cabinets.

Grace located the remote and tuned it to an eighties station, mostly to serve as a reminder of how she ended up there in that kitchen. Madonna, asking the all important question, "Who's That Girl?"

"I don't know. I just don't know," Grace answered back.

She'd sent Nick out to the car for her bag, thankful that at the last minute she'd remembered to pack a couple of cookbooks. She wasn't sure she had the presence of mind to remember anything but her name right now. And even that was fuzzy.

She figured she'd start with some salted herring and a rich meat soup called *solyanka* for the first course. For a main dish, she'd chosen *golubtsy*—cabbage leaves stuffed with ground beef, rice and vegetables—easy to make but very tasty. And she'd decided to finish it off with a simple Ukranian honey cake.

An hour later, she was so engrossed in cooking she didn't even hear Tina clatter into the kitchen on her stilts.

"What are you doing?" Tina said.

Grace flung the cup of dried beans she was measuring in the air, and they rained down on the granite countertop like black hail. "Jesus. You scared me."

"Nervous type, huh?"

"Just a little."

The young woman chewed a long, red nail. "You don't look like Nick's kind of girl."

"So I've heard." Grace collected the spilled beans and swept them into the garbage disposal.

"Where'dja meet him?"

"Caligula."

"Ah. Eighties night." Tina nodded, as if that explained everything.

Grace put a hand on her hip. "Did you want something?"

"Nope."

Tina examined her cleavage and pulled a bra strap out from beneath the tank top, adjusting the slider before letting it snap back into place.

She was pretty, in a little-girl-in-the-big-wide-world kind of way. Nice skin, clear blue eyes. What was a pretty young woman like her doing with a pig like Skobelov?

Grace shook her head and turned back to the beans.

Tina slid onto a chair at the table, a massive golden oak affair with six chunky chairs. She straightened a leg and wiggled her ankle. "My dogs are barking. You mind if I take off my shoes?"

"Be my guest. I don't know how you can walk in those things."

"It sucks. But Viktor likes them. So do the men at the club."

"The club?"

"The Cat's Meow. I'm a dancer."

Aha. That explained it.

After a while, Grace said, "So how did you get into that line of work?"

Tina shrugged. "Just lucky, I guess. I was in my senior year of high school when I met this guy who ran a club. He said I had a good look, and I could make a lot of money. Way more than working at the mall or waitressing or something. So I started dancing on the weekends, and I eventually just quit school. I mean, what was the point? I figure I can always get my GED when my boobs start to sag."

Grace looked down at her own chest. She wanted to say, "That'll come sooner than you think," but she knew it was futile. The road to thirty was a long, slow, bumpy ride, and then after that it was nothing but freeway. You sped toward middle age doing ninety, stopping only for more and more frequent bathroom breaks.

"So what do you do?" Tina said.

"I'm a mother." Grace's tone was defensive, she knew, borne from years of comments like "Oh, well. That's *okay*." Or, "Don't worry, you can always have a career when the children get a little older." People tended to look at stay-at-home mothers as if their heads were freakishly large or they were covered in boils.

Since when was being a mother such an easy job?

It wasn't. It was a lot like being a wilderness survival guide. She'd like to see those tight-ass executives sticking their hands in the toilet to remove a Barbie head, or reading *Goodnight Moon* seventeen times in a steam-filled bathroom with a coughing infant.

She sighed. "I'm a mother," she said again, this time without all the venom.

"Cool," said Tina. And she looked as if she actually meant it.

Grace could have hugged her.

She whisked a few eggs in a bowl and slowly added some flour, blending it to form a sticky dough. She turned the dough out onto a floured board and began to knead.

"You need some help?" Tina said.

"You can cut up that cabbage if you want."

Tina jumped up from the table and came over to the counter. "Where are the knives?"

"You don't know? I thought you lived here."

"I do, but, Viktor has a girl come in to cook a couple of nights a week. The rest of the time we eat at the club. I don't really cook."

"That's a shame. It can be very relaxing."

"Yeah?"

"Sure. Here, I'll show you."

For the next hour, Grace showed Tina how to chop vegetables, roll out dough and measure spices by using the palm of her hand. And as they cooked, the two met on that age-old common ground. Busting on their men.

"You should have seen him with that car," Grace said. "Every Sunday without fail, out in the garage rubbing it with a diaper. He imported his car wax from Australia."

Tina snorted. "You're exaggerating."

"Nope. He wouldn't even touch the thing without wearing a pair of white gloves. He looked like Mary Poppins."

"Yeah, well I got a good one about him." She jerked her head toward the television room."

"What's that?"

"He never misses an episode of *The Golden Girls*."

"You're kidding. *The Golden Girls?*"

"Yep. I think he has the hots for Bea Arthur." Tina chopped quietly for a moment. "I don't sleep with him, you know."

"It's really none of my business."

"He just keeps me around for show. Likes people to think we're a couple. But he's into weird stuff, ya know?"

"I got that impression."

Tina shrugged. "You wouldn't believe some of the shit I've seen."

Grace was suddenly queasy. "Is there any wine around here?"

Tina put her hands on her hips. "You know, you've got nice boobs. I have a shirt that would look great on you."

She practically skipped from the room, and Grace

smiled. It was nice to have someone to talk to. A distraction.

She pulled the Ukranian honey cake out of the oven and put it on a wire rack to cool.

Tina was a good listener. She had a natural curiosity, asking all kinds of questions, and Grace wondered if maybe Tina was feeling unsettled with her life. Maybe wishing she was doing something more than dancing on a pole.

But, hey. At least she had a job. Grace had no idea what she'd be doing for money a couple of months from now. Maybe she'd be wishing for a pole and for anyone interested enough to watch her dance on it.

She hoisted her boobs higher. Maybe she could spend some of her settlement on some implants and get in on the Mammoth Mammary action at the Cat's Meow.

Tina came back to the kitchen with an armload of clothes, which she dumped on the kitchen table. She picked out an electric-pink wraparound blouse and held it up to Grace as she stirred the pot of *solyanka*.

"What do you think?" Tina said.

"It looks kind of…revealing for me."

Tina rolled her eyes. "You gotta advertise, Grace. Believe me, not many women have such a nice rack." She rooted through the pile and came out with a pair of pink and gold leopard-print pants.

"I don't know…"

"What?"

"Leopard print? It's not really me."

"It's cheetah. And animal patterns are classic. They never go out of style. You know why?"

Grace shook her head.

"Because they make women feel wild. Like they're hard to handle. Don't you want to feel wild sometimes?"

"If you only knew."

Tina rummaged through the pile again, digging out a pair of hot-pink high-heeled stilettos. "I brought shoes, too. It looks like we're about the same size."

"Tina, I appreciate the gesture. But—"

Tina snatched the wooden spoon from Grace and shoved the clothes in her arms. "Go on. Go try them on. The bathroom's that way."

Sunday, 9:45 p.m.
Little Red

The bathroom looked more like a day spa, complete with massage table, pedicure chair and several stainless steel gadgets that could have been some sort of weird torture devices.

The room was bigger than her bedroom, with dark marble floors and an entire mirrored wall. The white whirlpool tub on the far side seated four. Or one big, fat Russian.

A double-wide white chaise lounge rested in the corner atop a fuzzy white rug, with an overflowing basket of magazines beside it. *Vogue*. *Cosmopolitan*. *Us*. *People*.

Grace shed her own carefully chosen clothes and folded them neatly before slipping on the pink wraparound. She fastened the buttons, pulling the blouse tightly across her chest.

It was a top not constructed for those who wore a bra.

She removed hers and refastened the shirt, enjoying the newfound freedom. She couldn't remember the last time she'd gone without a bra. Probably at the same EarthSavers outing where she hadn't showered.

She squeezed into the cheetah-print pants, which had apparently been constructed of some miracle space-age fabric able to stretch enough to accommodate her more generous proportions. But there, too, underpants were *vestis non grata*.

She doffed her panties and stuffed them into the pocket of her folded pants, as she did at the gynecologist's office. Because, of course, unlike a full-on assault by the parts they covered, her underthings would be an affront to a gynecologist's delicate sensibilities.

Clothing in place, she slid her feet into Tina's shoes before turning to face herself in the mirrored wall. For a second she thought there was someone else in the bathroom with her. Then she realized that wild woman in the mirror was *her*.

She smoothed the blouse over her belly and turned from side to side, marveling at the way Tina's clothes hugged her curves and the way the high heels shaped her calves. Though she never hesitated to show off her legs, lately she'd taken to wearing loose shirts and baggy jackets to hide the rest of her.

This getup didn't leave much to the imagination. And, she thought with satisfaction, that was okay. As long as she could stay here in the bathroom.

True, no one would ever mistake her for a model or actress, but she didn't look too bad. She wondered what Lorraine and Misty and Brenda would think if they saw her in this getup.

It would definitely *not* get her invited to the Christmas party.

She took one last look at herself and gathered up her clothes. On her way out of the bathroom she ran into Nick in the hallway.

He gave a low whistle. "Look at you." He ran a finger over her jawline and down her throat, stopping just before he reached her cleavage. "Smoking clothes, baby."

She leaned in for a fix of Aramis, coming dangerously close to bursting into flames. "Tina lent them to me."

"Nice."

For a split second he morphed into the wolf in the story of Little Red Riding Hood.

My, what big teeth you have.

She backed away slowly. No sudden moves. "Dinner will be ready in a few minutes. Think Mr. Skobelov is ready to eat?"

Nick laughed. It was a low, sexy sound that went straight to her toes. "He's always ready to eat."

"Right. Good. Okay." She tried to ease by, but he stood right in the middle of the hallway, forcing her to brush up against him.

He stuck out an arm and blocked her from passing, brushing his lips against her earlobe. "Let me tell you what *I'm* hungry for."

Then he whispered something so sinful, so physically convoluted and deliciously amoral, she couldn't even repeat it to herself.

She fanned herself with her hand, wondering if the laws of physics would even permit such a suggestion.

"Listen," she whispered. "I know you want Skobelov to think we're together. I understand that. But we aren't. So keep your… your *appetite* to yourself. Okay?"

She teetered off toward the kitchen in Tina's high heels, praying her knees would hold her up, at least until she was out of his sight.

CHAPTER 15.5

Sunday, 9:56 p.m.
Little Red Redux

Did he hear that right?

Pete adjusted the volume on the receiver. He wondered where Nick came up with this stuff. But more importantly, he wondered what Grace was wearing to elicit such a creative proposition.

Damn.

He shouldn't have let her go in there.

No, that was just Little Petey talking. He wanted Grace. Didn't want Balboa to have her.

Balboa was the type of guy who always got the girl. And Pete was the kind who pretended he didn't care. But he did.

Especially with this girl.

She was what his mother would call "well crafted," both inside and out. Intelligent, funny, beautiful. The kind of woman who didn't notice men like him.

That was the story of his life. He was the guy all the girls wanted in high school—for a lab partner. The kind all the girls wanted in college—for a buddy.

He suspected his ex-wife had married him because he made her feel safe. He took care of her. Held her arm when they crossed the road. Checked out the house when she heard noises at night. But in the end, it wasn't enough.

She'd divorced him and married a karate instructor.

He hadn't even attempted to date since then. The past two years had been consumed with the Skobelov investigation, so there hadn't been much of a conflict. But now. Now, there was Grace.

He sighed and unfolded the papers he'd found in her purse in the hotel room. Release forms from a pharmaceutical distribution company for a large amount of Viagra to be shipped to an address in Lodi, California. But why would Grace have them?

He didn't even want to think about it.

His cell phone rang, and he flipped it open.

"Yeah, Lou."

"Morton's on the move."

"Great. Stay with him. Let me know where he ends up."

"Will do."

The toilet flushed in Pete's ear, and Balboa started humming again. Pete rubbed his eyes. He couldn't wait for this assignment to be over. He'd had about all the dealings with Nick Balboa he could take.

CHAPTER 16

Sunday, 10:48 p.m.
Fighting Squirrels

"What did I tell you? You look great." Tina turned Grace around in the kitchen and examined her from every angle. "How do you feel?"

"I have to admit, I feel pretty good. Just like you said. Wild. Sexy."

"Uh-huh. And the guys couldn't take their eyes off you at dinner."

"I've got news for you. It wasn't *me* they were looking at. It was the girls, here." She hefted her bra-free bosom.

"You. The girls. What's the difference?"

Grace sighed. "I don't want to get attention that way. It's wrong."

Tina looked hurt. "You saying what I do is wrong?"

"No. It's just wrong for me."

Tina shook her head. "Lots of people judge me, ya know. They think I'm some kind of slut. But I'm not. I'm a dancer. And just because I'm proud of my body and I show it off doesn't mean I don't respect myself."

"I didn't mean to… I'm sorry, Tina. I'm not judging you. Really. I guess I'm just not comfortable putting myself out there like that."

"But you said yourself you feel good. What's wrong with that?"

"I don't know."

What *was* wrong with that? She hadn't always been so uptight about her body. When she was young—and much closer to perfect—she'd had no qualms about showing a little T and A. But now that she was older, now that her body had gone through perfectly normal changes, she was ashamed of it. Well, that just sucked.

Meanwhile, most men could walk around in a Speedo, with a package that jiggled like fighting squirrels and a belly like the Pillsbury Doughboy, and wouldn't think twice about the way they looked.

It just wasn't fair.

Grace and Tina loaded the dishwasher and scrubbed the pots in silence.

Nick came into the kitchen. "Well, you did it, baby."

"Did what?"

"Viktor. He loved the food."

"Yeah, he did," said Tina. "I haven't seen him so happy since he stopped having his back waxed."

"Eew."

Nick wrapped his arms around her waist and pulled her close. "Bottom line is you bought us some more time. Good job."

Tina gave her a questioning look, which she ignored. She had no idea how much the young woman knew about Skobelov's business, but she sure wasn't going to be the one to clue her in on anything. The less Tina knew, the better.

Ditto for herself.

Grace peeled Nick off of her. "That's great. But we've got to clean up in here."

Nick nodded. "Viktor and I are gonna go out for a while. You two girls behave yourselves."

"Oh, goody." Tina said. "I want to do Grace's makeup."

Grace gave her a smile she hoped looked a little more enthusiastic than she felt. "Can't wait."

Sunday, 11:29 p.m.
Tattoo You

Tina's bedroom was done up in gold brocade and black lacquer, with a king-size bed, her own bathroom and a

217

walk-in closet that would have housed a family of four in New York City.

She hustled Grace into the bathroom, sat her down in front of the mirror and poured her a glass of wine from a bottle she'd retrieved from a little refrigerator near the tub.

"Isn't this fun?" She picked up a hairbrush and started teasing Grace's hair. "When I was little, I got this big Barbie head for Christmas that you could put makeup on and fix her hair. I loved that thing."

"Maybe you'd be a good cosmetologist or a makeup artist."

Tina smiled. "You really are a mother, aren't you?"

"Can't help it."

"So what was all that about with Nick? What did he mean that you bought him more time?"

"He's working on a project for your…for Mr. Skobelov, and he needed a little more time."

"What kind of project?"

"I'm not sure, really. I don't ask."

Tina nodded. "I hear you. I don't really want to know about Viktor's business, ya know? What should we do with your eyes?"

"Do we have to do anything? Aren't they okay the way they are?"

"Don't be chicken. How about some Wild Heather eyeliner?"

"Sounds wonderful."

Apparently, Tina didn't get the sarcasm in her tone because she tilted Grace's head back and started penciling purple along her lids.

While her neck was busy cramping up, Grace thought she'd ask a few questions of her own.

"So how did you hook up with Viktor?"

Tina popped her gum. "I guess I just got lucky."

"Hmm. Yeah, but how did you meet him?"

Tina hesitated. "A mutual friend introduced us."

"Ah." Nick. It had to be. How many people had told her Nick preferred a girl like Tina?

"Are you from Philadelphia?"

"Uh-uh. Baltimore." Tina selected some eye shadow from her makeup case and held it up beside Grace's eyes. "Misty Mauve or Irish Rose?"

Because she wanted nothing more than to get her nose out of Tina's cleavage, she muttered, "May as well stick with the flower theme and go with Irish Rose."

"Good choice."

It seemed so odd to hear someone say that. She didn't feel like she'd made a good choice in quite a while. Most certainly not this weekend.

A good choice would have been to keep her simple hairstyle. A good choice would have been to say no to Tom when he'd asked her to sign the papers.

A good choice would have been to pick "truth" instead of "dare."

Well, hell. She'd made what she'd thought were good choices her whole life. Majoring in marketing when she really loved dance. Marrying Tom when she'd been enjoying her freedom.

Natural childbirth.

In retrospect, they'd all left something to be desired. But at least they'd *seemed* like good choices at the time. Responsible choices.

The choices she'd made this weekend? Well, they hadn't even seemed good when she'd made them, but at least they made life a hell of a lot more stimulating.

"I doubt the guys will be home anytime soon," Tina said, looking at her watch. "How about a henna tattoo?"

Hmm. A henna tattoo? Not a good choice.

"Go for it."

Tina grinned. "I like you, Grace."

"I like you, too."

Tina rooted through a makeup case the size of a steamer trunk and pulled out her henna kit.

She poured Grace another glass of wine. "After we do tattoos, I'll teach you some dance moves."

"Can't wait."

Monday, 6:43 a.m.
Bungee Jumping

Momentary panic engulfed Grace when she opened her eyes to the dark red chain links encircling her bicep.

Had she met a sailor in Tina's bathroom? Had she joined the Navy?

Then she remembered. The tattoo wasn't real. Unlike the nasty headache, which definitely was.

She had to stop drinking. Really.

So far this weekend alone, she'd given away her panties and a twenty-thousand-dollar ring, made out with two complete strangers, agreed to cook for an insane Russian mobster, got a tattoo and learned how to dance like a stripper. What was next? Jumping out of a cake at a bachelor party? Bungee jumping naked off the Betsy Ross Bridge?

She dragged her ass out of bed and down the hall to the bathroom, where she splashed some cold water on her face and caught her reflection in the mirror.

She looked like a psychotic raccoon.

She grabbed her cell phone out of the charger, which she'd thankfully remembered to bring, and slunk out to the kitchen. No one else was up, which didn't surprise her. Nick and Skobelov hadn't returned until after three, and Tina had drunk as much wine as she had.

If the batter for the blini she planned to make this morning didn't have to rise twice, she wouldn't be up herself. But she had to hold up her end of the bargain—distract Skobelov with carbs and butter.

It seemed silly, but she didn't want to let Pete down.

She wondered if he and Louis had located the computer key yet. From the conversation she'd overheard last night between Skobelov and Nick, time was running out. The Russian was getting antsy, and no amount of *rasstegai* or *solyanka* was going to help.

She had to admit that Skobelov scared her, more than just a little. It was less what he said than how he said it. Less how he looked at her than what she saw in his eyes. Nothing. Absolutely nothing. Not a touch of humor. No forgiveness. Not a modicum of understanding or compassion.

He was like a sadistic little kid with a magnifying glass, and everyone else was just an ant on the sidewalk. Everyone near him walked around in fear, wondering when they were going to get fried. Even Nick seemed a little intimidated.

Grace wondered what had made him decide to become an informant. He had to know what would happen if Skobelov found out.

She finished the blini batter and removed a package of smoked salmon from the refrigerator. It tasted better at room temperature. Then she boiled the eggs for the *okroshka* she planned to make for lunch.

At 8:01 a.m. she decided it was late enough to call her mother.

She poured another cup of coffee and settled into the breakfast nook with her cell phone. When she flipped it open, she saw that she had a message from Tom. She punched in the access code for her voice mail.

"Gracie, where in the hell are you? I need to talk to you. I need those papers. Call me, please."

His typical composure, and the clipped diction that had first impressed her and then later driven her crazy, were gone. He sounded on edge. Nervous, even. And Tom didn't get nervous.

She called his cell phone, but he didn't answer. She refused to call his home phone. No way did she want to talk to Marlene.

Besides, he really wasn't going to be happy when he found out that she no longer had the papers and wasn't sure where they were.

She hit the speed dial for her parents' number.

"Hi, Mom."

"Grace! I left a couple of messages on your home phone. Did you get them?"

"Actually, I haven't been home. I spent the night at a friend's house."

"A friend?"

Did she detect a note of disapproval in her mother's tone?

A *note?* Hell, it was more like an entire symphony.

"Yes, a *friend*. Her name is Tina."

"Oh, do I know her?"

"No. I'm pretty sure you don't."

"What does *she* do?"

Ever since her mother had gone back to work part-time at the Wicks 'n' Sticks in the mall, she'd become a real career woman.

"She's, ah...she's in the entertainment business."

"Oh? What, like the record business or something?"

"No. Dinner theater."

"Interesting. Maybe your father and I could go see her sometime. We love the theater, you know."

By "the theater" her mother meant the First Presbyterian Players' production of *Oklahoma*.

"I'll try to get you tickets. I'm sure you'd enjoy the show. How are the kids?"

"They're fine. Megan is on the phone all the time, though. Did you know she talks to boys?"

"I suspected as much."

"And you approve of that?"

Grace sighed. "Mom, if I could have, I would have kept them all in diapers for the rest of their lives. But they have to grow up, don't they? Whether we like it or not."

Her mother was uncharacteristically silent for a moment. "I suppose they do."

Grace had no doubt her mother was remembering *her* in diapers and wondering where the years went. She could hear the nostalgia seeping through the quiet hum of the phone line.

"I love you, Mom," Grace said.

"I love you, too."

"Can you keep the kids one more night? Take them to school tomorrow morning? I'll pick them up after."

"Of course, dear. I know you have a lot on your mind."

"You have no idea."

CHAPTER 16.5

Monday, 8:22 a.m.
Champagne Hangover

Pete fell out of the chair in which he'd fallen asleep listening to Balboa's snoring, after Balboa had apparently fallen asleep in Skobelov's living room with his face right near the bug.

Pete picked himself up off the floor and wiped the drool from the corners of his mouth, stumbling toward the kitchen to make a pot of coffee.

He loaded the filter to the brim. The blacker the better.

Maybe he could just skip the middleman and snort the coffee grounds instead.

He guessed that Nick would be asleep for a few more hours at least, considering the night he'd had at the Cat's Meow. A night that yielded absolutely nothing in the way of usable information against Skobelov but plenty of moans and sighs from the ladies giving lap dances in the Champagne Room.

The Russian must have been licking his wounds from the Eagles' loss to the Giants and brought Nick along for the ride. Literally.

Unfortunately, Pete had been stuck in his car in the parking lot with the body wire receiver all night, with nothing to think about except what Grace might be doing back at the apartment.

At least he hadn't been worried about her safety. With Nick and Skobelov at the Cat's Meow, there wasn't a whole lot to worry about.

He yawned and wondered if he had enough time to take a shower before Nick woke up. He checked to make sure the feed from the bug was being recorded and trudged upstairs, coffee mug in hand.

Just before he stepped into the shower, his cell phone rang.

"Yeah?"

"It's Lou. Morton's on the move. He left the chippie in the hotel room and he's driving into Jersey in a little rented piece of crap. Friggin' tin can with wheels."

"He heading north or south?"

"North. Could be going to New York."

"Nah. I don't think so. If he had business in New York,

why wouldn't he have flown into New York? Why would he be staying near Philadelphia?"

"You seen the price of a hotel room in New York?"

"Maybe he's got something set up with Johnny Iatesta in Trenton," Pete said.

Lou was silent for a minute. "Makes sense. Iatesta does a good business with counterfeit credit cards."

"Yeah. And the state police in Jersey have been on him for immigration violations. Fake social security cards, that kind of thing."

"Think Morton's trying to get a bidding war going between Iatesta and Skobelov?"

"That would be my guess. Just stay on him, okay? Let me know what happens."

"Right. Later."

CHAPTER 17

Monday, 9:30 a.m.
Charo's Blouse

When Grace got back to her bedroom after taking a shower, Tina was sitting on her bed, her wallet in hand.

"Oh, sorry." Tina blushed. "I just… I thought you might have some pictures of your kids. I didn't have any brothers and sisters growing up, and I—"

"It's okay. Here." She took the wallet from Tina and opened up a little snap to reveal an accordion of snapshots. "This is Megan, my oldest. And this is Kevin. He's ten. And this is Callie, my youngest."

"This your husband?" Tina pointed to a picture of Tom standing beside his Corvette.

"My ex. Yeah."

Tina had a funny look on her face.

"What's the matter?"

"Nothing." She sighed. "I just wonder if I'll ever have that. A husband and a family and all that. Dancers don't have the most stable lives, ya know?"

Grace sat down on the bed beside the younger woman. "You don't have to be a dancer forever."

Tina smiled. "Thanks, *Mom.*"

"What can I say? Dress me like a wild woman, but underneath I'm still a mother."

"Speaking of wild women, what are you going to wear today?"

Grace pulled a pair of chinos and a lavender scoop-neck T-shirt out of her bag.

"No, no, no-o-o." Tina stuffed the clothes back into her bag. "That shirt won't even show your tattoo. Come on, I'll fix you up."

"You don't have to do that, Tina. Really."

"Oh, I don't mind. I have tons of clothes. Viktor really spoils me that way. He likes me to look good."

"Yeah, but—"

Tina grabbed her hand and pulled her off the bed. "I'll do your hair, too, while we're at it."

Grace bit her tongue.

She wouldn't pooh-pooh an offer of help in that area. She guessed the trade-off for hair that didn't have a brush tangled in it would have to be clothes that looked like they'd been worn in a Whitesnake video.

Tina led her down the long hall and into her own bedroom, disappearing into the huge walk-in closet. Grace sat down on the bed—which she was surprised to find neatly made—and examined her surroundings.

There seemed to be very little of a personal nature in Tina's room. No framed photographs on the nightstand. No bric-a-brac. No jewelry lying around.

"How long did you say you've lived here?" Grace said.

Tina's voice sounded as if it were coming from a cave. "About six months, I guess."

"Where did you live before that?"

"Here and there. Nowhere special." Tina emerged from her closet with several garments draped over her arm. She held up the clothes. "I found the perfect outfit for you."

Grace eyed the blue lamé rhumba blouse and black cigarette pants. "Wow. That's something else."

"Isn't it? I'll get you some shoes."

Grace held the ruffled blouse up to her chest and looked in the mirror.

"Did you get this shirt off of eBay or something? It was Charo's, right?"

"Who's Charo?"

Grace shook her head. At least she wouldn't see

231

anyone she knew. It was unlikely Misty or Brenda or Lorraine would be walking around this part of town.

"Cuchi-cuchi," she muttered beneath her breath.

Monday, 11:44 a.m.
Lucky

In the middle of breakfast, the phone rang.

Skobelov, his mouth stuffed with blini, looked at Nick.

"You want me to get it?" Nick said.

Skobelov nodded.

Nick wiped his hands on his pants and picked up the phone. "Yo."

He listened for a while and then put his hand over the mouthpiece of the phone. "It's Morton," he said to Skobelov. "He's in Philadelphia. He wants to meet you. Says he got an offer from Johnny Iatesta for the files and wants to give you a chance to make a counteroffer."

"I already paid him. What? He offer me my own damn property now?"

"I'll take care of it," Nick said.

"No. You take care of enough already. I have another thing for you." Skobelov wiped his mouth.

"Another thing?" said Nick.

Skobelov pointed to the phone. "Tell him I'll meet him. At the club." He looked at his watch. "Two o'clock."

Nick put the phone to his ear. "He says he'll meet you. Two o'clock at a club called the Cat's Meow, on Cottman Avenue. You got a car? Okay. Okay."

Nick hung up the phone. "He'll be there."

Skobelov nodded.

"You sure you don't want me to go with you?" Nick said.

"Nah. You blow this once already. I got another job for you." Skobelov motioned to Tina. "Get me pen."

He scribbled on an envelope and handed it to Nick. "You know this guy. Go get him. He is being very difficult. I need to talk to him."

Nick looked at the envelope and then at Grace.

She raised her eyebrows.

Nick gave her a little shrug. To Skobelov he said, "Where do you want me to take him?"

"To the club also. Today I take care of two assholes at once, no?" He laughed and stuffed his mouth with another forkful of blini.

"I'm going with you, Vik," Tina said. "I have to work at three." To Grace, she said, "You wanna come along?"

Grace's cell phone rang, and she pulled it out of the back pocket of the cigarette pants.

"Hello?"

"Don't go." Pete's voice was low and calm. "Make an excuse."

She hesitated. "Okay. I'll be sure to do that."

"Call me back after they leave."

"Will do. Okay. Bye."

She closed the cell phone and it slipped out of her nervous hands, skittering beneath the table. She went down on her hands and knees and crawled under the table, coming face-to-face with the Russian's fat knees.

Figured. He had two different-colored socks on.

She retrieved the phone and resurfaced.

"Who was that?" Tina asked.

"Oh. My mom. She wants to borrow my, uh…my lobster pot."

"You got a lobster pot?" Tina said.

"Sure, doesn't everybody?"

Tina shrugged.

Skobelov looked at Nick. "What you waiting for?"

Nick hesitated and looked at Grace.

"You hump your girlfriend later, eh? Go."

Nick gave Grace one last, lingering look as he left the kitchen.

"So, you wanna go with us or what?" Tina asked Grace.

"Actually, I think I'll hang out here. Do the dishes, get a start on dinner. Is there anything special you want, Mr. Skobelov?"

The Russian rubbed his jaw. "You make *pelmeni?*"

"Of course. It's my specialty."

Skobelov smiled, showing tiny brown teeth that looked like dried mung beans. "Nicky is lucky man."

"Why?" Grace said, completely forgetting that she and Nick were supposed to be an item.

Skobelov laughed, but Grace caught Tina staring at her, an unidentifiable look in her eyes.

Not for the first time, she wondered if Tina might not be as ditzy as she pretended to be.

A few minutes later, Grace watched from the window as Skobelov's long black Cadillac emerged from one of the oversized doors of the building's four-thousand-square-foot garage. From her vantage point, she could see Benny the Brick Wall driving. She wondered if there was anyone guarding the desk in the lobby or if she was all alone in the building.

Not a comforting thought.

She ran into her bedroom and locked the door before picking up her phone and dialing Pete's number.

"Yeah." Pete's voice nearly made her sob with relief, and she realized just how insecure she'd been feeling without him around.

"They're gone."

"All of them?"

"Nick, Skobelov and Tina. And a guy named Benny was driving them. I don't know if there's anyone else in the building."

235

"Good. Get your stuff together. It's time to get you out of there. I'll meet you out at the corner in ten minutes."

"Right."

She stuffed her cell phone in her purse, on the verge of tears. She didn't know if it was because she was relieved to be leaving or sad that she wasn't going to make *pelmeni*.

Probably both. It felt good to cook for people who really appreciated it, even if they were felons.

Monday, 12:26 p.m.
Ch-ch-changes

On her way out the door, Grace realized she hadn't changed. She was still wearing Tina's clothes.

Well, it was too late now.

She doubted Tina would miss them, but she still vowed to somehow get the clothes back to her.

She wondered if Tina would get arrested along with Skobelov and felt a pang of regret for the younger woman, whose only mistake had been to give in to the lure of a tampon-factory penthouse and a Frederick's of Hollywood credit card with no limit.

Grace gave the place one last look and locked the door behind her, admiring the Michelangelo again as she waited for the elevator. Which didn't come.

She pushed the button again, but then noticed she needed a key to operate the elevator.

Crap.

An examination of the little vestibule revealed a door that led to a dim, concrete stairwell.

Noise echoed eerily off the putty-colored cinder block walls, making her own breathing sound like a pit full of vipers. At ground level she peered through the narrow glass window, out into a deserted lobby.

The heavy door groaned on its hinges as she emerged from the stairwell. She took shallow breaths, waiting for someone to pop up from behind the desk like an over-size jack-in-the-box with multiple piercings and a scary clown tattoo.

But the place remained quiet as a…well, as a deserted tampon factory. She hustled to the door she and Nick had entered, past the camera mounted above the desk. The bright sunlight outside threw her. Though she knew it was only midday, it felt as if it should be dark. She'd been at Skobelov's for less than twenty-four hours, but it had felt like a week.

Resisting the urge to look behind her just in case someone was watching, she hung a right and walked calmly to the corner. A chilly wind made the ruffles on the Charo blouse dance, and she realized she'd forgotten her coat in the hall closet.

A bright-pink flier skittered up the sidewalk and pasted itself to her leg. She bent down and peeled it off her calf. A two-for-one special at Paco Taco.

She crumpled it up and then realized she didn't have any pockets, so she bent down and unzipped the duffel and stuffed it in.

When she stood up, Pete's Taurus was driving past.

"Hey!"

His car jerked to a stop and then backed up. He unrolled the passenger side window.

Her stomach did a little flip.

He leaned over on the seat and said, "Sorry. I didn't realize that was you."

"You were looking right at me. Who did you think it was?"

Two bright spots of color emerged on his cheeks. "Never mind."

She opened the car door and threw her bag into the backseat before sliding in beside him in the front.

"You look…different," he said. "Is that a tattoo?"

"Tina gave me a makeover. What do you think?"

"I think the 'Chiquita Banana' girl wants her shirt back."

CHAPTER 17.5

Monday, 12:28 p.m.
Wet Dreams

Pete had to fight to keep his eyes on the road.

What was she wearing?

He wasn't lying when he said he didn't see her back there. What he'd seen was the stuff of his adolescent wet dreams—a cross between Carmen Miranda, Cheryl Ladd and a Times Square hooker who would do anything for fifteen bucks.

The ruffly shirt was killing him.

"Where are we going?" she asked.

"Back to my place. We have to wait to hear from Nick."

"Isn't he wired?"

"Yeah, but he's way out of range. Besides, he's nowhere near Morton, and that's who we're interested in."

"Who's Nick with?"

Pete debated how much he should tell her.

Just then his phone rang. Saved by the bell. Or rather, by the sound of Wild Cherry.

"Yeah."

"It's Lou. Morton's leaving the motel."

"Okay. Keep me posted. I'm going to drop Grace off at my place. Let me know when he gets to the club."

Pete felt a rush of adrenaline. This was it. The payoff was so close he could practically taste the celebratory champagne.

As soon as he had Skobelov, Morton and the memory key in the same place at the same time, his case would be made. With Nick's corroboration, the wiretap and bug recordings, along with some physical evidence, they'd get the Russian on numerous fraud and identity theft charges.

Soon, all of this would be a memory.

He looked at Grace in her ruffly shirt and thought about how some things would be much easier to remember than others.

Of all the cases he'd worked, none had been as aggravating, or as interesting, as this one. And the "interesting" part was largely due to the woman sitting beside him.

It was going to be tough saying goodbye to her. He reached over to touch her shoulder as she looked out the window, but snatched his hand back before he made contact.

Jesus. When had he turned into such a schmuck? Maybe it was time to seriously consider retiring. When a man couldn't let go of a case without an ache in his gut, something was seriously wrong.

CHAPTER 18

Monday, 12:42 p.m.
Guy Talk

Pete dropped Grace's duffel inside his front door. "Here you go. I'll talk to you later."

"No way. I want to go with you."

Pete sighed. "You're imagining you're Nancy Drew again."

"Oh, come on. You can't just leave me here."

"You're right." He fished her keys from his pants pocket and dropped them into her palm. "Go home. But don't leave the country. I may need you later on."

"Pete—"

"I'm going to the Cat's Meow. If you show up there, how are you going to explain your presence to Skobelov? You didn't have a car while you were at his apartment."

She hesitated. "Good point."

"If things end the way I think they will, it could get dangerous, Grace." He touched her face. "You were a big help, but your part is over now."

She was worried about Tina, and Pete, too. And even a little bit about Nick. But she knew Pete was right. She was a mother, for God's sake. She should go home. Call her kids. Take a nice, hot bath.

She nodded. "Okay. Will you call me when it's over? Let me know how it went?"

"Won't Nick do that?"

"Aagh." She growled with frustration. "For the last time, Nick is *not* my boyfriend."

But Pete was already smiling. "I know. He was wearing a wire, remember? I heard you send him packing."

He slid his fingers over her cheek into her hair, pulling her close. His lips covered hers. His kiss took her breath away. She closed her eyes, and wrapped her arms around his neck.

The kiss seemed to go on forever. Pete ran a hand down her side and settled it on her hip. She leaned against him, but before she could get comfortable, he pulled away.

"I have to go."

"You're leaving me here alone?"

"I trust you. Just make sure the door is locked when you leave."

She nodded. "Be careful."

"I will. Go home."

"I will."

He gave her one last, quick kiss, and then he was gone.

She stood there for a moment in Pete's small foyer, letting her heart settle into a regular beat. It seemed as if she'd been on edge for so long, she wondered if her adrenaline levels would ever be normal again.

She decided a drink of water might help slake the seemingly unquenchable thirst she'd had the whole weekend.

In the kitchen, red lights glowed all over the receivers on the table, and Grace knew from watching Lou that they were recording whatever was going on in Skobelov's living room and on Nick's wire.

She grabbed a glass from the cabinet beside the sink and ran some tap water in it. While she was drinking, the receiver for Nick's wire let out a startling squawk.

Grace dropped the glass into the sink with a thunk.

Nick must have just come back within range of the receiver.

She heard his voice over the receiver. "Grace has them. They're in her purse. I saw them."

"When did you see Grace?" said another voice. A defensive voice, with neat, clipped diction.

Tom.

Could Tom be the guy Skobelov had sent Nick to pick up?

She knew Tom was acquainted with Nick, but with Skobelov? Why? How?

She hurried over to the receiver, straining to hear the conversation that was interrupted by fits of static.

"...no big deal. We met at a club."

"Wasn't that a coincidence?" Tom said, a note of suspicion in his voice.

"Listen, man. I'm trying to help you. Skobelov isn't happy with you."

"You're sure Grace has the papers?" Tom said.

"She did Friday night."

There was a long silence. Then Tom said "Did you hook up with my wife?"

"Wouldn't that be your *ex*-wife?" Nick said. "And why shouldn't I hook up with her? She's hot."

Grace couldn't help but smile. What she wouldn't give to see Tom's face at that moment.

"You goddamned sh—"

"Relax, man," Nick said. "I just wanted to talk to her about a business proposition."

"A business proposition? What the hell?" Now Tom was getting out of control. "If you've dragged my wife into something—"

"Hey. Let's not talk about this right now, okay?"

"Bullshit. We are going to talk about it."

"I'd advise against it," Nick said.

"I don't care what you'd advise against, you *a-hole*."

"A-hole?" Nick sounded amused. "Okay, then, *Tom Becker*. Let's talk about it." Nick spoke slowly and clearly. "If you don't deliver the shipment of Viagra you promised Skobelov, you better kiss your ass goodbye."

Silence, and then Tom's voice, quiet and tired. "Christ. How did I ever get into this?"

The Viagra wasn't for Tom, Grace realized. It was for Skobelov.

And she suspected it wasn't for his personal use. She wondered exactly how much Viagra those papers were meant to release.

Hadn't Pete said that Skobelov was involved in all kinds of things? Things like Internet drug sales, maybe?

How *had* Tom gotten into that?

Goddamned Marlene. She'd bet on it. Marlene and her insatiable desire for designer clothes and five-star vacations. And Tom was just stupid enough to do it for her, too.

"Listen," she heard Nick say. "We'll swing by Skobelov's. Grace is there. You'll get the papers, show them to Viktor, tell him you'll have the stuff by Monday, and that's that. No big deal."

"Grace is at Skobelov's?" Tom had gone from defeated to incredulous.

It was amazing how much emotion you could hear in somebody's voice. She'd never realized how much before. Then again, she'd never listened to conversations over a body wire before.

And that's when she realized that the whole conversation Tom and Nick just had—the one where they discussed her forging papers and Tom's involvement in procuring Viagra—had been recorded.

Was *still* being recorded. Right there, in Pete's kitchen.

She dove for her phone and dialed Tom's cell number. It rang once, twice, three times—a ring she couldn't hear over Nick's wire—until finally someone answered.

"Hello?"

Shit. Marlene.

"Hello? Hello!"

Grace closed her eyes and counted to three. "Marlene, it's Grace."

"Oh. Grace. Tom isn't here."

"I know. I need to get a message to him. It's urgent—"

"Urgent. I see." Marlene sighed. "Grace, aren't you tired of all the theatrics?" Marlene spoke slowly and calmly, as if she were dealing with an escaped mental patient.

"Marlene, listen to me. If Tom calls, you have to tell him—"

"I'm sorry, Grace. I don't have to tell him anything.

I'm not your messenger girl, and I refuse to let you drag me into the middle of your problems."

Wha-a-at? Grace's mouth fell open. "Excuse me, but you *created* my problems when you decided to coat yourself in jelly and roll around on my good Ralph Lauren sheets."

Marlene sighed again. "Must we point fingers, Grace? Do we have to rehash that scene over and over?"

"I'm not reha—"

"I can't believe you're so petty."

"So *petty*? Are you *kidding* me?" *Breathe. Breathe. Breathe.* "Listen, Marlene. If Tom calls you, just tell him to call me on my cell phone as soon as possible."

"Right. I'll tell him it's *urgent.*"

"You little—" A very bad word came to Grace's lips, but before she could release it into the cellular universe, Marlene had already hung up.

Grace squeezed the phone, imagining it was Marlene's wrinkled little neck.

Think, think.

She wished she had Nick's cell phone number, but she didn't.

She could call Pete, but then what? She would have to tell him that Tom was working with Skobolev—that is, if he didn't already know.

"...want to get her involved," Tom said.

What?

Grace turned up the volume on the receiver.

"I mean, she's the mother of my children," Tom went on. "I never should have asked her to sign those papers."

"Hey," said Nick. "Why not? She's got a God-given talent. Why not have her use it?"

"That's what you were going to do, wasn't it?"

"Listen," Nick said. "I was just gonna capitalize on an opportunity. What's wrong with that?"

"What's wrong is that Grace is a good person. I didn't tell you that stuff about her so you could recruit her for some scheme. I just...I just wanted you to think I was, you know, cool. That I understood all this underworld crap because I had a wife who'd done time for forgery." Tom sighed. "If I'd have known you would try to use her..."

"Like you did?" Nick said.

"I really have been a shit." Tom's breathing came heavy. "I pretty much forced her into signing those papers. I used my kids' security as a carrot. I'm such an asshole."

Imagine that. Tom wasn't as big a prick as she'd thought.

She bit her lip to keep from crying.

"So, what? You don't want to go get Grace?" Nick said. "See if she has the papers?"

"No. Just take me to Skobelov."

Monday, 12:52 p.m.
In the Grinder

No, no, no.

She couldn't let it happen. She'd seen Skobelov. She knew what he was like.

He was like a shark.

She shivered.

She had to get to Tom. Tell him to get out of the ocean. Stay away from the shark.

As soon as Pete arrested Skobelov, Tom would be out of danger.

Wait. Not true.

She looked at the receiver on the table. Everything Tom and Nick had just said had been recorded on the machine. Tom was in this way too deep to get out of it unscathed. There was no way to erase what he'd said. It was burned onto a CD.

She could take the disk, but she had no idea what else was on it or what might need to be recorded later. It could mean the difference between Skobelov getting what he deserved or getting away with everything.

She couldn't take that chance. She wouldn't endanger Pete's investigation.

But she could at least save Tom from getting his ass kicked by the Russian. As for her own ass, there was no doubt it would be in the grinder as soon as Pete heard those recordings.

She grabbed her bag and headed for the door, hoping she could make it to the Cat's Meow before they did.

CHAPTER 18.5

Monday, 12:52 p.m.
Tunnel Vision

Lou had already arrived at the Cat's Meow by the time Pete got there. He pulled into a spot near the end of the parking lot, next to Lou's Chrysler sedan, and took a deep breath.

This was it. This was *it*.

The Russian and Morton together under one roof, negotiating a price for thirty-thousand names and social security numbers.

But where in the hell was Balboa and his body wire? Without proof that this meeting had gone down, the event would be as believable as Bigfoot meeting the Loch Ness Monster. No matter how many witnesses there were, it was only a myth until hard proof could be offered up.

He couldn't take a chance that Balboa would be a no-show.

He popped the trunk latch for the Taurus and went around to the back of the car. Opening one of the large plastic containers, he removed a palm-size black box. Attached by a short wire to the box was a tiny camera lens, no bigger than the tip of a pen.

He taped the box to the inside of a black Flyers baseball cap and threaded the camera lens through a small hole, until it rested on the brim of the cap. It was virtually invisible against the black and orange lettering on the cap.

In the event that Nick didn't show, Pete would at least have video of the meeting. No audio, though. He didn't want to get too close.

He pulled the cap onto his head and adjusted the brim before setting up a small video receiver in the trunk and plugging it into a power inverter. He turned it on, and a picture of his trunk sprang to life on the screen.

He turned his head this way and that, checking to make sure the receiver picked up a clean signal when he moved.

When he was certain everything worked, he turned the recording device on and shut the trunk.

He smiled. He'd heard about this. The brass ring. The silver lining. The light at the end of the tunnel.

And in a case that had been nothing but a train wreck, that light sure looked good about now.

He just hoped the light wasn't attached to a train that was gonna hit him head-on.

CHAPTER 19

Monday, 1:15 p.m.
Warden

The parking lot was full. One-fifteen on a Monday afternoon, and the parking lot was friggin' full.

Who *were* these men who hung out at a strip joint on a Monday afternoon?

She doubled back through the parking lot and around the rear of the Cat's Meow, taking a detour through the alley where Pete had caught her leaving the club the day before.

As she entered the alley, the back door opened and three men emerged. Two extra-large and one medium.

The first extra-large was Benny the Brick Wall, sporting a black cowboy hat, a scowl and a healthy bulge beneath the too-tight gray sport coat he wore. The

255

second extra-large was more monolith than a brick wall. He resembled a statue on Easter Island, broad and flat and seemingly chiseled out of stone.

And the unfortunate medium being muscled along between them was—

Oh, boy.

It was Tom.

As she drove past, Grace ducked down as far as she could behind the steering wheel. But like typical men, they weren't looking at her, they were looking at the Beemer. That marvel of German engineering.

She'd like to put a 540i on stage in the club and see which the boys were more likely to ogle—half-naked girls or thirty-seven-hundred pounds of sculpted steel.

Whether or not Tom recognized the car as hers was anybody's guess. She imagined he was pretty nervous. But if he *had* recognized it, or her, he'd given no outward indication.

She cruised past and watched in the rearview mirror as the three men disappeared into the building across the alley from the club.

Damn. That couldn't be good.

She circled the lot again, forced to wait until a guy in a pickup truck lit a cigarette, dialed his cell phone and fiddled with the radio before finally giving up his parking spot.

Heels clicking on the macadam, she hurried into the alley. Now the Cat's Meow was to her right, and the building where Benny and his Easter Island friend had taken Tom was to the left.

She debated what to do. Should she try to go into the Cat's Meow and get help? But who would help her?

Nick? He was the one who'd brought Tom here in the first place.

Pete? She wasn't even sure he was here. But even if he was, she doubted he'd be willing to mess up his investigation to save her ex-husband's ass.

And that left...

Nobody.

Nobody but her.

Tom's ass was in her hands.

She shuddered at the thought. But still, she had to do *something*. After all, he may have screwed up royally but he was still the father of her children.

She veered left, edging her way along the tan corrugated siding until she reached a narrow slit of a window, about chin high, that stretched for about three or four feet. She tried to look in, but the window had been covered with brown butcher paper from the inside.

She made it to the door and pressed her ear against the cold metal, but she couldn't hear a thing through the industrial-weight door. She rattled the door handle, which was, of course, locked.

Now what, Nancy Drew?

The answer was simple. Knock. But she needed something first.

She searched the alley until she found what she was looking for. A small square of cardboard the size of a playing card. She slipped it down the front of her blouse and pounded on the door.

No one answered.

She pounded again, harder.

Benny opened the door a half minute later, minus the cowboy hat but still wearing the scowl. The light of recognition flashed in his bulldog eyes.

"Hi. Benny, isn't it? I'm looking for Nick Balboa. Is he with you?"

"No, he ain't with me. Get outta here." He started back in.

"Wait! Can you tell me where Nick is?"

"Not my turn to be his babysitter."

Nice guy.

Benny disappeared and the door swung shut, but not before Grace was able to get the cardboard in between the door and the latch, so it closed but couldn't lock.

Now all she had to do was wait until Benny had gone back to whatever it was he'd been doing.

As she waited, her bladder sprang to life the way it always did when she played warden with the neighborhood kids. Warden was a rather sadistic, preteen version of hide-and-seek, played in the dark with flashlights over a whole neighborhood block. One kid would be the warden, the others would be inmates who'd escaped from prison. The prisoners would have to hide and, once in a spot, could not leave that spot until they were found or called in for dinner by their mothers.

Without fail, Grace would have to pee almost as soon as the game had begun. She'd sit beneath a shrub in torturous pain until she finally had to quit and run home.

Wouldn't it be great if she could run home right now? But that was, of course, out of the question. This time, she was the warden.

So she opened the door and stepped into what appeared to be some sort of evil genius's laboratory.

Monday, 1:28 p.m.
WWCAD?

A machine that looked like an oversize roller-coaster car sat in the middle of the floor, surrounded by a low scaffolding platform. The row of fluorescent lights hanging above it were unlit; a noisy humming sound emanated from the thing, as if it were growling at her.

Tall shelves that stretched from floor to ceiling, loaded with boxes of unidentifiable content, lined the long wall beside it. A chemical odor hung in the air, reminding her of the smell of her fourth-grade classroom after the teacher had handed out freshly mimeographed math quizzes.

Just as stupid women in horror movies will do, instead of turning tail and running, she wandered farther in and let the door close behind her.

The place was dim except for a flood of bright light spilling over the floor from an open doorway at the end of the wall. An occasional shadow broke the strip of light, and she knew from watching too many detective shows that that had to be where she would find Tom.

She pulled off one of Tina's shoes, testing the heft in her hand, slashing the spiked heel down in front of her like a butcher knife.

Not bad. She could definitely put an eye out.

She removed the other shoe and crept toward the light, avoiding the growling monstrosity in the center of the cold cement floor. After what seemed an eternity, she reached the door. She flattened herself against the wall and leaned in, peeking around the doorjamb.

The room was a small office, furnished only with a couple of filing cabinets, a chrome-and-particle-board desk and a battered chair on wheels. Tom sat on the chair, elbows resting on the desk, his head in his hands.

His right eye was centered in a big red circle, which was sure to become a big black circle by tomorrow. A small trickle of blood had escaped his nose.

It looked like Benny and his friend had wasted no time.

Suddenly, the machine let out a big, long hiss and went quiet. The place turned eerily silent. The kind of silent where you think you might have died and just didn't know it yet, and you wanted to make some noise—any noise—to prove that theory wrong.

Grace jerked away from the doorway and stood completely still, her heart pounding painfully in her chest.

"Finally," Benny said from within the office. "I hate that friggin' noise. Now, where were we?"

"Our friend was gonna call his distribution center," said the other simian. "Weren't cha?"

"No," Tom said. "I wasn't. I told you, I don't have the authority to release large amounts of pharmaceuticals. Not without an order from a legitimate distributor and a signed release form from my boss. And I can't get that. At least not today."

"Like I said," Benny said, "Every day Mr. Skobelov's clients have to go without the valuable medication you supply, they suffer horrible anguish. Do you know what it's like not to be able to bone your girlfriend?"

"I could hazard a guess," Tom said.

He could? Grace idly wondered if he'd ever had trouble boning Marlene.

Yuck.

"And everyday Mr. Skobelov's clients can't get the

medication they need is one more day Mr. Skobelov's reputation suffers. Which means *you* have to suffer. Understand?"

"I get it," Tom said. "But I'm telling you, there's nothing I can do. The procedures have changed. I don't have access to the stuff anymore. I'm afraid I'm going to have to bow out of this deal."

Benny and his friend yukked it up, as if someone had just told a joke about a rabbi, a priest and a duck going into a bar.

"He's gonna hafta bow out," said Benny.

"Yeah," said the monolith. "Bow out."

"I'll tell you what," said Benny. "Why don't I help you *bow out.*"

Grace heard the wheels of the chair squeak and then a pounding sound she suspected was Tom's head bouncing off the desk.

She grimaced.

"Zat a good bow?" Benny asked. "You like that?"

Tom groaned.

Grace moved into the doorway, brandishing her size eight pumps. Unfortunately, the simians had their backs toward her, which completely blew her big entrance.

Even more unfortunately, Easter Island had one of Tom's legs in his hand. Benny raised a foot and stomped on it, and there was a sickening crack.

Grace stumbled away from the door. Now would be the time to do something, wouldn't it? Now would be the time to ask *WWCAD?*

What Would Charlie's Angels Do?

Clearly, this situation called for a distraction.

Where was Farrah Fawcett and her little white tennis skirt when you needed her?

The sound of Tom's groans making her increasingly nervous, Grace scanned the warehouse for something, anything, she could use to create a diversion.

She circled the machine, locating a control desk on the far end with about sixty lit buttons and a network of switches and levers. The word *Heidelberg* stretched across the top of the machine in silver letters.

Heidelberg? Why did that sound familiar?

She figured one of the buttons had to turn the thing on, so she began pressing them.

The machine roared to life with an earsplitting squeal, hissing and groaning even louder than it had before.

Within seconds, Benny and Easter Island shot from the office. The looks on their faces would have been comical if they hadn't been spattered with blood.

The blood that, by rights, was *hers* to spill. And if she'd managed to restrain herself from spilling it through fourteen years of marriage and a venomous divorce, it wasn't fair that they'd gone and done it.

The two men ran toward the machine. Grace circled it, and when they'd reached the control panel she waved at them from the other end.

"Hey. Over here." Her voice echoed through the building.

The simians charged, coming at her with speed that belied their blocky physiques. Before she could get out, they got between her and the door, trapping her inside the warehouse. With a sick feeling growing in the pit of her stomach, she realized her mistake.

Faulty math.

While there were three Angels, there was only one of her. On the show, the bad guys always had to split up to chase the Angels, but in this case it was two on one.

Which, if she remembered simple fractions correctly, two on one gave her only half a chance to get away.

CHAPTER 19.5

Monday, 1:36 p.m.
Lassoed

Pete sipped his coffee and tried to keep his eye on the dancers, instead of on Skobelov's booth in the back of the club.

The Russian's girlfriend had just left the table, so Skobelov was there with Morton, Ferret and Balboa, who had arrived about ten minutes ago. As long as he kept his cool and kept the camera trained on the Russian's table, they'd have enough to prove the two were dealing.

One of the dancers, a girl in a Wonder Woman costume, hopped off the stage and tried to lasso him with her gold rope. A bunch of young guys in the corner cheered. But Pete wasn't worried about being noticed at the Cat's Meow. He'd frequented the club for nearly six months now, getting to know the regulars and the girls, making himself inconspicuous by his habitual presence.

That's how he'd gotten to Balboa. And that was how he was going to nail Skobelov.

Lou was seated at the bar not ten feet away from the Russian's group, tucking dollar bills into a dancer's G-string and, presumably, keeping tabs on what was happening.

Lou had a tiny receiver in his ear that would pick up the sound from Balboa's bug, so he could monitor the conversation. As soon as Lou gave the signal, Pete would call the cops for backup.

Wonder Woman left him and climbed back up on stage, shedding the gold bustier she'd been wearing to reveal a set of red tassled pasties.

Pete felt bad for the girls. Most of them were really sweet, just hard workers trying to feed their kids or pay the mortgage or send money home to their families in other countries.

When Skobelov was taken down they'd all be out of jobs, since the Russian owned the club. But there wasn't anything Pete could do about that. It was an unfortunate side effect of his work.

But it wouldn't be an issue after today.

Pete had already decided it was time to retire. Get a civilian job, maybe start up a security consulting business. Buy that 1965 Mustang he'd always dreamed about.

He moved the baseball cap slightly, lining up the eye of the camera with Skobelov's big blob of a body.

He was close now.

So close.

CHAPTER 20

Monday, 1:39 p.m.
Boneheads

They were close. So close.

The simians charged. Grace retreated.

She flew past the open office door—where Tom lay on the floor, groaning—and around the perimeter of the building, desperately searching for another way out of the warehouse.

Benny and Easter Island split up, coming at her from opposite sides. Apparently, they weren't as dumb as they looked. *They* understood division.

She was trapped.

She backed up against the shelves on the wall, groping for the tire iron that according to all cheesy detective show scripts should conveniently have been there.

It wasn't.

The only things on the shelves were a bunch of boxes.

If this were an episode of *Charlie's Angels* and she was Jill Munroe, those boxes would conveniently be filled with knives, or marbles or tiny goon-seeking missiles.

They weren't.

They were filled with paper.

Easter Island was still chugging his way around the machine, but Benny was close. Too close.

She had to do something fast.

Grace couldn't go right or left or down. The only way to go was up. She started up the shelves, but Benny reached her before she was out of range.

He grabbed her ankle. She gave him a kick, drilling him in the temple with her high heel. He let out a squeal that didn't sound like anything issued from a man his size.

She reached the top shelf and wedged herself behind the boxes, crawling on her hands and knees like a hamster in a tube. She could hear Benny, and now the monolith, too, pacing beneath her.

Okay, now what?

She reached into one of the boxes and pulled out a handful of paper.

She could throw it. Maybe cause a wicked paper cut.

Alright. No. That was ridiculous.

She looked at the paper in her hands. Blue, with red circles. Familiar.

Was it…?

She squinted at it in the dim light.

Damn. It was.

Sheets and sheets of Social Security cards. There had to be thousands of them.

And then she remembered what Heidelberg was. A company that manufactured printing presses.

Somebody was making their own Social Security cards.

Her stomach rolled. She didn't want to see this. Didn't want to know about it. She just wanted to get out of there and get some help for Tom.

At the moment it seemed unlikely, considering the fact that she had roughly five hundred pounds of goon below her, waiting for her to come down.

What she needed was the element of surprise.

Closing her eyes, she said a little prayer. Then she pushed one of the boxes over the edge of the shelf with her shoulder.

It landed with a thunk.

She looked down over the edge to see Benny sprawled on the ground, surrounded by a pool of blue paper.

Bull's-eye!

The monolith looked up at her, stunned.

She let another bomb drop. It missed the mark but sent the goon scrambling for cover.

She clambered down the shelves and bolted for the door, not daring to look behind her.

She imagined she could feel hot breath on the back of her neck as she burst into the alley and sped toward the club.

The cold air seared her lungs as Easter Island chased her around the Cat's Meow for the second time. She realized she couldn't risk trying to get to her car. If he caught up with her in the parking lot, she was dead meat.

She lost him around the corner, and once she had a decent lead on him, ducked into the front door of the club.

"Twenty bucks, please," said the bouncer.

Damn.

"I don't have any money," she said. "I mean, I'm a dancer. I'm new, and I'm late for my shift."

"You're a dancer?" He looked her over. "You look a little ol—"

"I have a specialty. Ya know?" She winked at him but suspected it looked about as cute as the spastic cat's eye winking on the roof.

"I guess." But he looked like he didn't guess at all.

"Can I go in?"

He shrugged and held the door open. "Break a leg."

She shuddered.

Inside the club, she walked straight into a table while her eyes fought to adjust to the dark. A cold draft of air at her ankles told her someone else had just entered the small vestibule in the club, and by the way her hair stood up on the back of her neck, she strongly suspected it was Benny's friend.

Keeping to the shadows on the outskirts of the room, she made her way toward the back door.

She had to get help. Poor Tom. God only knew what damage those thugs had done.

Benny's friend emerged at the front door and squinted into the darkness. He set off in the opposite direction from her, toward Skobelov's booth.

Grace spotted Louis at the bar. She tried to get his attention, but his eyes were glued to the women on the stage.

Wasn't he supposed to be working?

Men.

She couldn't just go to him, either. Easter Island was sure to see her if she got near the lights of the stage.

She walked past the row of booths and through an area of freestanding tables, where a rowdy bunch of young guys—college students, she guessed—had camped out. Empty beer pitchers and shot glasses littered the tables.

The guys made catcalls at Grace as she passed.

They had definitely met their two-drink minimums.

"You going on next, honey?" one of the kids yelled to her. A kid who looked a lot like her nephew.

A kid who *was* her nephew!

"*Michael?*"

The kid belched. "Aunt Grace?"

"Jesus!" Grace made a beeline for the table. "What are you doing here?"

"I…" He glanced sheepishly at the stage. "Uh, it's for a report."

Grace gave him the sternest face she could muster. "Michael, how did you get in here? You're underage. Your mother would kill you. Not to mention Grandma."

Another kid walked over. "Hey, Mike. Who's the MILF?"

"Dude, chill. This is my *aunt*." Michael shook his head. "Man, what a bonehead."

"What's a MILF?" Grace said.

The other kid grinned. "A Mother I'd Like to F—"

"*Dude*," Grace said.

Michael plopped into a chair. "You gonna tell my mom, Aunt Grace?"

Grace sighed. "No. Just… No more beer for you. Drink some water. A lot of water. And get out of here right now."

He pointed at his friends. "But I came with them, and

they aren't gonna want to leave until they see the one who dresses like Supergirl."

"Gotta stay for Supergirl," the other kid agreed. "She's the best. She does this thing with her kryptonite that'll blow your mind."

Michael looked up at Grace with bleary eyes. "We'll leave right after that, I promise."

"Is there a designated driver?" Grace asked.

Michael shrugged.

Grace looked around for Easter Island, but he had disappeared. "Don't go anywhere with anyone. I'll handle this."

"Cool." Michael went back to his table with the rest of the boneheads, and Grace made a beeline for the back hallway.

She wound her way through the serpentine corridors, trying to remember how to get to the back door. The club music thumped, reaching decibels that could rival the noise from the Heidelberg next door.

And suddenly Benny was there, plugging up the hallway as effectively as a cork in a bottle of wine. He must have come in through the back door.

Fortunately his back was to her, and she slipped into the ladies' room.

And let's face it. At that point, it wasn't the worst place she could hide.

Monday, 1:59 p.m.
The Justice League

When Grace peeked out into the hall again, Benny was gone.

She crept along the maze of hallways, wishing she had a compass. Or better yet, OnStar navigation system.

Hello ma'am, can I help you? the perky-yet-soothing OnStar voice would say.

Yes, I'm trying to get to the alley, but I'm afraid I'm a little lost.

Well, we can certainly help you! Just make a left at the storage closet, a right at the alcove that smells like a dead rat and go straight through the section of hallway painted that lovely shade of earwax yellow.

After a few minutes of aimless wandering, Grace passed a door that looked familiar.

The changing room.

She slipped inside, thinking she might find a cell phone or maybe a Sherpa who could guide her out of the place.

A dark-haired dancer in a blue silk robe stood in front of the mirror, applying her lipstick.

"Excuse me…" Grace said.

The dancer turned. "Grace?"

"Tina! I didn't even recognize you."

"It's the black wig. What's going on? You look like hell."

Grace burst into tears. "This Easter Island guy broke Tom's leg, and Michael is here and he shouldn't be here, and Benny's after me and I'm scared. I can't help it. I tried to be brave but I'm done. I'm just scared."

"Wait. Hold on a minute. Who's Tom? Who's Michael?"

Grace's breaths came in fits and starts. "Tom, my ex-husband. I don't know. Somehow he's involved with Viktor. And Michael is my nephew. He's underage, shouldn't be here, but he is. He's right out there! I—"

"Shh. It's okay. Tell me again about Tom."

Grace sank into one of the folding chairs. "He's across the street, in this big warehouse. Benny and some other guy took him there and beat the crap out of him. I'm pretty sure they broke his leg. I'm afraid they're going to kill him. And me."

Grace stopped. Why was she telling Skobelov's girl-friend all of this? It was crazy.

But it wasn't. Because right now, Tina was the only person she had any hope of trusting. The only one who could help her.

Tina handed her a tissue. "You say Tom's across the alley?"

Grace nodded. "In the warehouse, in the back office."

"And your nephew, where is he? What does he look like?"

"Curly brown hair, Temple University sweatshirt. He's with a bunch of frat boys on the left side of the club."

Tina pulled off her wig and tossed it on her dressing table. "Okay, just stay put. I'll take care of everything." She gave Grace a quick hug and hurried out the door.

Grace grabbed another tissue and blew her nose. She took a few cleansing breaths to try to stop her hands from shaking.

Tina would help her. She had to.

A door off to her right—one she hadn't even noticed before—burst open. Grace nearly fell off her chair. Music blared as three dancers hurried into the changing room, and Grace realized the door must lead directly to the stage.

"What a crowd today," said one of the women, a short blonde in a Batgirl costume. She spoke with a thick accent and looked as if she couldn't be a minute older than sixteen. "I dance my tits off, and for what?" She pulled a handful of dollar bills out of her underwear. "Ten…eleven…twelve. Twelve dollars. I could have stayed home and watched *When Harry Met Sally* on cable."

"It's all those freakin' college students," said another, an unnatural redhead dressed as Aquagirl. "They expect you to let them cop a feel every time they put a dollar in your pants."

An older, more worldly looking Catwoman who was at least twenty-three, shook her head. "Some days just suck." As if she'd just noticed Grace, she said, "You better get going, girl. The natives are getting restless."

"Oh, I'm not…My shift hasn't started."

The girl shrugged.

"Hey, do any of you have a cell phone?" Grace asked.

"They don't work in here," said Aquagirl. "Don't you know this is the pit of hell?"

The others laughed.

"There's a pay phone in the hall," one offered.

"Great. Anybody have a couple quarters I can borrow?"

The girl with the accent handed Grace one of the dollars she'd pulled out of her G-string. "You'll have to get change."

Grace thanked her and went to the door that led into the hallway, opening it just a crack. Benny stood less than two feet away.

Damn.

She closed the door softly. If he decided to poke his head in there, she was a goner. She was trapped like a rat in a trash can.

No, that wasn't quite true.

She looked at the stage door.

There was another way out.

CHAPTER 20.5

Monday, 2:02 p.m.
Chernobyl

"Su-per-girl. Su-per-girl." The kids in the back chanted at the empty stage.

Usually Pete enjoyed Masked Mondays. It was something a little different, watching the surrogates of his boyhood fantasies come alive onstage. But not today.

Today, he'd already had all the excitement he could handle, and then some.

His chest squeezed, and he wondered idly if he might be having a heart attack. Even if he was, it wouldn't matter. He was gonna sit right there in that chair, still as stone, until Lou gave him the goddamned signal.

"Come on, Lou," he muttered under his breath.

At Skobelov's table, things were heating up.

The Russian wore a flat look, which Pete knew from experience was his look of rage. His Chernobyl look.

Morton, oblivious to the impending explosion, continued to shake his head. Pete tried to focus on Lou instead of the unfolding scene, but he found he couldn't look away.

Skobelov leaned back in his seat and looked at Nick.

Nick leaned forward and spoke to Morton, who shook his head again.

Skobelov's goon moved to the table and stood behind Morton.

Pete held his breath.

He willed Morton to back down. The man couldn't testify with his balls in his throat.

Skobelov turned redder and redder. Borscht-red.

Morton said something else, and Skobelov smiled. He waved his goon off and lit a cigar.

Pete wiped the sweat off his forehead with his sleeve. Morton would live to see the next minute, at least.

From the corner of the club, a cheer went up.

Supergirl had arrived.

CHAPTER 21

Monday, 2:05 p.m.
Kryptonite

Grace stumbled into the light, tugging at the sequined bra that barely covered her boobs.

In the corner the boneheads cheered wildly. She prayed Michael was no longer among them. Wasn't there a law against letting your nephew see you in a G-string?

This was insane.

All the other stuff—giving Nick her panties, cooking for Skobelov, trying to save Tom—that stuff was crazy. But this? This was certifiably insane.

"Psst. Hey, Supergirl. You forgot something." A dancer just off the stage tossed Grace a big, blue, phallic-looking chunk of plastic.

Grace caught it in one hand. "What is it?"

"Your kryptonite."

Another cheer went up from the frat boys.

You should see what she does with her kryptonite.

"Ugh."

Music blared over the speakers behind her, but beyond the lights she could see anticipation in the eyes that stared up at her. They were waiting for her.

Actually, they were *waiting* for Tina, but they were gonna *get* her, at least for a minute or two. Just until she could make sure Benny and his friend weren't around and she could get off the stage and get out of this place.

She hoped the black wig she was wearing changed her appearance as much as it had changed Tina's.

She shimmied out to one of the poles as the music changed from pulsing techno to a sensuous rhythm-and-blues thing with lots of sax. She scanned the faces in the crowd, spotting Benny in the crowd.

He squinted at her as if trying to figure out how he knew her, and she realized if she didn't start moving soon, he'd figure it out pretty quickly.

So she closed her eyes and grabbed the nearest pole, leaning her back against it so she didn't pass out or fall over or something.

Grace did a couple of squats and then spun around and hooked an elbow around the pole, spinning until she was dizzy. She opened her eyes a crack and saw that the men at the bar along the stage were looking at her as if they expected something more.

Benny had moved closer, and she began to panic.

Her movements felt stiff, even to her, and she suspected she looked something like a corpse humping a pole. She forced herself to loosen up. Go with the flow. Listen to the music.

She'd done this before. Tina had taught her all the moves in the big white bathroom at Skobelov's place. She'd done fine there, and she could do it again.

But the lights, the music, the eyes. They conspired against her.

She knew then that she was about to relive one of the most embarrassing moments of her life. A humiliation so acute, it had taken many dozens of cupcakes to repair the damage to her reputation at William Marker Elementary School, and several month's worth of therapy later in life to repair the damage to her psyche.

It was the fourth-grade talent show, and she had forgotten every single step of the jazz dance routine she'd practiced for months. So she'd ended up performing the only dance she could remember at the time—the one the kids on the *Brady Bunch* had done for *their* talent show when they'd sung that groovy song "Keep On."

The humiliation had been utter and complete.

And now, in a horrifying echo of that day, she did the only moves she could remember.

Yoga poses.

She threw the kryptonite on the floor and sank to her knees, striking the lion pose. To her surprise, the crowd cheered. Maybe because her left breast had nearly popped out of her bra.

But, hey, it had worked.

She transitioned into cobra pose and then rolled onto her back, bringing her feet over her head into plow pose. The crowd cheered again.

Who knew yoga could be so sexy?

Getting into it now, she did the full sun salutation sequence into scorpion pose, standing on her elbows, back arched, her legs dangling above her head.

"Hey, come on over here, honey!" a guy called from the bar. She crawled over to him on her hands and knees, retrieving the kryptonite on the way and rubbing it sensuously over his bald head. The crowd went wild.

The guy stuffed a couple dollar bills into her bra, and she almost punched him until she remembered she was supposed to be grateful.

She scanned the room again and noticed that Benny had moved back by the DJ booth.

She struck a shooting bow pose before crawling along the edge of the bar. More bills were stuffed into places she didn't want to think about, before she finally made it to the edge of the stage and dropped down to the floor.

It was now or never.

She started off toward the front door, but just then Easter Island materialized there. His beady little eyes came to rest on her, so she danced toward the tables.

Easter Island moved closer.

She turned her back to him, and straddled the lap of a guy wearing a Flyers cap.

"Not now, honey." He tried to push her off.

"Hey, cowboy. Don't you want a special dance?"

The guy tensed. "Grace?"

Oh, my God.

"Pete?"

"What in the *hell* are you doing here?" he growled. "What's with that getup?"

"I—"

"Wait. No. I don't even want to know. Just get the hell out of here, right—"

"Freeze! Everybody stay where you are!"

Men in uniforms and blue jackets poured in through the front door and from the back hallway, surrounding the stage and the DJ booth, blocking the exits.

"God *damn* it," Pete swore.

"What? You didn't call them?" Grace said.

Pete shook his head. "I don't even know if we got what we needed yet."

Grace's stomach turned. She could have made a wild guess as to who had called the cops. She looked around but didn't see Tina anywhere.

Much to her relief, Michael was gone, too. A few police officers had rounded up the boneheads and were checking their IDs.

Numerous police officers and a group of men in dark blue windbreakers with the letters USCIS emblazoned in yellow on the back surrounded Skobelov's booth.

Grace's close proximity to Pete—and she couldn't get much closer than straddling his lap—allowed her to see the anger and disappointment in his eyes.

She took his face in her hands. "I'm sorry."

And she really, truly was.

Pete shook his head. "It's not your fault. Just bad luck." He lifted her off his lap. "By the way, you look pretty hot."

"You think?"

"Definitely."

He left her standing there and went over to where Louis was talking to the men in the blue windbreakers.

"Ma'am?" An officer approached her. "You're going to have to come with me."

"But I'm not a dancer. I don't really work here."

He glanced sideways at her. "Yes, ma'am."

"No, I'm serious!" She reached up and tugged the black wig off. "I don't work here."

"Yes, ma'am."

She sighed. "Can I at least get the money out of my bra? It's itching like crazy."

The cop led her through the hallway and past the changing room, where the other members of the Justice League were also being fitted with beautiful plastic bracelets. Most of them were speaking in rapid-fire Russian.

Grace and her escort soon emerged into the alley, which was jammed with police cars and vans and dark blue government-issue vehicles.

The door to the warehouse next door was closed, taped over with yellow crime tape.

The cop led her by the arm toward one of the police vans—the paddy wagon, she guessed—but before they'd reached it, the door to one of the unmarked cars swung open.

"Wait," said a female voice. "I'll handle her."

Tina emerged from the backseat of the vehicle, wearing jeans and a blue windbreaker. She gave a low whistle. "Look at you. Taking the wild thing a bit far, aren't you, Grace?"

Grace's mouth fell open. "Are you...?"

Tina nodded. "U.S. Citizenship and Immigration Services."

Grace shook her head. "That explains a lot. Did I ruin your case, too?"

Tina looked confused. "No, you didn't ruin our case. We had to move a little early, but we were ready."

"I guess you found Tom." She nodded toward the warehouse.

"Yeah." Tina took her to the car.

Grace got into the backseat and Tina slid in beside her.

"Your ex-husband was in pretty bad shape. They took him to Penn."

Grace's stomach churned. "Is he going to be okay?"

"I talked to the EMT. She said his vitals were relatively stable. He was hurting, but he should be alright. You cold?"

Grace nodded.

Tina grabbed a USCIS windbreaker from the front seat and wrapped it around Grace's shoulders. "Your nephew is back at the dorm safe and sound, probably sleeping it off."

"Thank you. I don't know how I can ever repay you."

Tina smiled. "Cook me dinner sometime?"

"Absolutely. And then maybe afterward we can play charades. I bet you'd be good at it."

Tina winked. "You're a good woman, Grace Becker. Promise me you'll be careful who you get involved with in the future?"

Grace nodded. "I will."

Tina opened the car door. "Wait here. I'll go get your stuff out of the club."

CHAPTER 21.5

Monday, 3:14 p.m.
Home Videos

Pete scoured the club for Grace, but she was nowhere to be found. Some of the dancers had been taken out of the club by Immigration Services, and he was worried Grace had been picked up along with them.

But when he'd spoken to the guy in charge for the USCIS, he couldn't locate her. Ditto for the Philly PD.

And he hadn't even said goodbye.

Once Pete had spoken to Lou, he discovered that they'd managed to get all the evidence they needed. Skobelov had agreed to pay Morton eighty thousand dollars for the memory key, topping Iatesta's bid of seventy grand.

Most of the conversation had been caught on Nick's

wire, as well as on the video feed in Pete's cap. At least it was, up until the point Grace had sat on his lap and blocked the action.

Man, he couldn't wait to get a look at that recording. A vision of Grace in that scorching Supergirl costume flashed through his mind. A vision he had to get out of his mind, pronto, unless he wanted to find himself sporting wood for the walk out to the parking lot.

He shook his head.

He was glad it was over, but he wasn't looking forward to the next few months.

Now, the grunt work for the case began. Submitting evidence, writing reports, working with federal prosecutors to build a case against Skobelov.

At least there would be no problem with that. Especially since somebody had located a counterfeiting operation across the alley, with a printing press, boxes of counterfeit Social Security cards and an office full of papers with Skobelov's name all over them.

How Pete and Lou had never gotten wind of the counterfeit operation was a mystery. And why Balboa had never told them about it was something that would definitely be addressed when they discussed his cooperation in the case with the prosecutor.

Lou came over and clapped Pete on the shoulder. "How 'bout a drink and some dinner?"

"Nah. I got a lot to do."

Lou nodded. "Guess I should get to work, too. Besides, nothing's gonna taste as good as Grace's cooking."

"Yeah."

"That Grace was one hell of a woman, eh boss?"

Pete rubbed the back of his neck. "She sure was."

CHAPTER 22

Monday, 6:35 p.m.
Burn Baby Burn

Grace rubbed a small circle in the steam on her bathroom mirror.

All her makeup was gone. The henna tattoo had already begun to fade. And she had no idea how long it would take her to style her hair.

She sighed.

Goodbye, wild woman.

She bundled up in a thick white robe and slippers and scuffled down the stairs to make a cup of tea.

The kids' backpacks hung by the door, and a frisson of worry ran down her spine. What if Tom's conversation with Nick, the one that was recorded from the body wire, got her in trouble?

It seemed unlikely since the papers she'd signed had never actually been used, and were, in fact, missing. But still, it was a possibility.

She didn't regret not taking the CD from the recorder at Pete's house, though. Skobelov was a despicable and dangerous man, who had undoubtedly ruined many lives. He deserved to go to prison for a long, long time.

Grace had called the hospital, but they wouldn't let her speak with Tom until the police had a chance to interview him.

Grace took her cup of tea into the living room and lit a fire.

She was sitting on the couch debating whether or not she should call her lawyer, when the doorbell rang.

Through the peephole, she could see Pete's red hair and the collar of his trench coat. Her heart jumped.

He turned when she opened the door, and smiled.

"I didn't think I'd see you so soon," she said. Or ever.

"Yeah, well, I wanted to return a few things." He pulled her panties out of his pocket and dangled them on his finger.

She grabbed his wrist and pulled him inside the house, her cheeks burning.

"Thanks," she said, plucking the panties from his finger and stuffing them into the pocket of her robe. "Do you have anything else? Something a little more sparkly, perhaps?"

He produced her ring from his other pocket and slipped it onto her finger. He cupped his hand over hers, giving it a squeeze.

"Thanks for your help, Grace. I'm sorry if I was... Well, if I wasn't always a gentleman."

"You were fine. You were doing your job. Did you get everything you needed on Skobelov?"

He shrugged. "It didn't turn out exactly as planned, but we got enough to put him out of business. Along with the immigration violations and Internet drug sales, he's going away for a long time."

"What about Nick?"

"He's under witness protection until the trial. After that, we'll see. He's got some things to answer for with the USCIS, too."

"So you were working with Tina all along?"

"Actually, no. We didn't even know about the immigration investigation. It was purely a coincidence they wrapped up their case the same time we were finishing ours."

Grace wondered if she should tell him that it wasn't quite the coincidence he thought, but she decided against it. "How could that have happened? I mean, how could you all not have known about each other?"

"It isn't all that uncommon, to tell you the truth. Lots of times different organizations will be working on the same guy or the same group, and they don't even know it. It's the secretive nature of the business, I guess."

"Hmm." She stared at her anniversary band. "What's going to happen to my ex-husband?"

"I'm not sure. We'll have to go through the evidence, see what comes up. If he agrees to testify, things might not be too bad for him."

She nodded.

"By the way, his girlfriend was arrested on conspiracy drug charges, too. They just picked her up half an hour ago."

"Marlene?"

He nodded.

Grace smiled. Finally, a bright spot in all this mess.

Pete hooked her chin with his fingers and tilted her head until she looked into his eyes. "I have something else."

He reached into the inside pocket of the trench coat and pulled out an envelope.

She opened it and removed the papers inside. The bottom of her stomach dropped out.

"I know what they are, Grace," Pete said quietly.

She nodded. What could she say? She'd been nailed. She just hoped she and Tom wouldn't be in jail at the same time.

Her poor kids. She could only imagine what their lives would be like.

Friend: Hey Kevin, wanna go skateboarding on Saturday?

Kevin: Nah, I can't. Gotta go to Riker's Island and see my mom and dad.

Her eyes filled with tears. She'd really screwed up this time.

"Hey," Pete said, pulling her close and kissing her forehead. "As far as I'm concerned, I have no idea what those are. They're yours. Do what you want with them."

"Really?"

"Really." He brushed a tear from her cheek. "I know why you did it, Grace. And if anyone asks, I don't have any idea what Tom was talking about on that recording. But I hope you understand that nothing is worth this kind of risk."

"I know. Believe me, I know."

"And I suggest you don't leave those lying around."

She went to the fireplace and threw the papers in, watching as they curled and blackened and turned to ash.

Goodbye, house.

Pete came up behind her and wrapped his arms around her waist. She turned, curling her fingers in his hair and bringing his mouth to hers.

It was a make out session to rival the one she'd had with Robbie Freeman when they'd played seven minutes in heaven at Cecilia's fifteenth birthday party. She couldn't figure out what was making her hotter—Pete or the fire.

He pulled away and took a deep breath. "I forgot to

tell you. We found out that Skobelov isn't Russian after all. He's Polish."

She laughed. "I guess no one was really who they seemed to be in this mess, huh?"

"Nobody except you."

She looked away. "I don't know. I seem to have a little problem figuring out who I am, these days."

"You're the genuine article, Grace." He hugged her, resting his chin on the top of her head. "So what are you going to do now?"

She sighed. "I've been thinking about that. I decided I'm going to try and start my own catering company."

"You're quite a cook."

"Among other things." She smiled. Maybe the wild woman hadn't completely disappeared, after all. She kissed him again. "Want to come upstairs with me? I'll model these for you." She pulled the panties out of the pocket of her robe.

Pete turned the color of a tomato. "I shouldn't. I mean, I really shouldn't get involved with someone from the case."

She kissed him again and twirled the panties on her finger as she headed for the stairs. "Why don't you just pretend I'm someone else?"

True Confessions
of the
Stratford Park PTA

by **Nancy Robards Thompson**

The journey of four women through midlife; man trouble; and their children's middle school hormones—as they find their place in this world...

Available October 2006
TheNextNovel.com

REQUEST YOUR FREE BOOKS!

2 FREE NOVELS TO INTRODUCE YOU TO OUR BRAND-NEW LINE!

NeXt™

There's the life you planned. And there's what comes next.

A stunning novel of love and renewal...

Everyone knows sisters like the Sams girls—
three women trying their best to be good
daughters, mothers and wives. Then in one
cataclysmic moment everything changes...
and the sisters have to uncover every shrouded
secret and risk lifetime bonds to ensure the
survival of all they love.

Graceland

by Lynne Hugo

Available October 2006
TheNextNovel.com

There's got to be a mourning-after!

Saturday, September 22

1) Get a ~~dog~~ cat
2) Get a man
3) Get adventurous (go skinny-dipping)
4) Get a LIFE!

Jill Townsend is learning to step beyond
the safe world she's always known to
take the leap into Merry Widowhood.

The Merry Widow's Diary

by Susan Crosby

Just like a blue moon, friendship is a beautiful thing

Hoping to rekindle a sense of purpose, Lola resurrects a childhood dream and buys a blue beach house. When she drags three of her fun-loving, margarita-sipping friends out for some gossip and good times, they discover the missing spark in their relationships.

Once in a Blue Moon

by Lenora Worth

Available October 2006
TheNextNovel.com

Friendship is the daily special!

When her perfect life does a 360, Lauren's almost certain she's hit rock bottom. But when unlikely friendships develop at her favorite diner, Lauren learns that the only thing she's lost is the barrier to discovering her better half.

Her Better Half

by C.J. Carmichael

Available September 2006
TheNextNovel.com

HN59